AND THE MOON IS FULL AND BRIGHT

NIZ THOMAS

COPYRIGHT

And the Moon Is Full and Bright

Made in the USA
Published by Throughplace Publishing
throughplace.com
Text copyright © 2024 by Michael Nisivoccia
All rights reserved.

Cover and Layout copyright © 2024 by Throughplace Publishing
Cover design by Michael Nisivoccia / Throughplace Publishing
Cover art copyright © semenov80 / wolf / Depositphotos
Cover art copyright © twovectors / Dwarf planet Pluto / Depositphotos
Cover art copyright © sozon / aged paper sheet / Depositphotos

COPYRIGHT

Family Tree

CONTENTS

ALSO BY NIZ THOMAS

FOR A FULL LIST AND LINKS TO PURCHASE, VISIT:

NIZTHOMAS.COM/BOOKS

NIZPATCHES

Volume One: Crime Stories

Volume Two: Twisted Crime

NIZ THOMAS COLLECTED

Volume One: Crime Stories

THE LEDGERMAN SERIES

The Omega Diner: A Ledgerman Story

Razor's Edge: A Ledgerman Novel

Thin Air: A Ledgerman Story

Last Ride: A Ledgerman Novel

THE TRUE NAME SERIES

Call Me Betsy

Call Me Gertrude

Call Me Aileen

NOVELS

Family Tree

Door Number Five at the Memory Motel

And The Moon Is Full And Bright

Election Day

SHORT STORIES

A Refraction of Kind Light

A Void of Ascendant Light

Becalm This Mighty Sea

Burn Off

Burn Together

Cheers

Elder Hunger

Fiona's Mercy

First Light of Every Morning

How to Commune with a Futurist

Lady Death

Lane Change

My Bleeding Kansas

No Control

Paint It Thrice

Rail Music

Ray-Ray's Stoop

Recidivist History

Red Tempest

Ships in the Night

Songbird

The Bad Guy

The Climb and The Glory

The Forever-ish Flame War

The Imminent Fire

The Impassable Way

The Light Alone

The Two O'Clock Killer

The Voice of Rage and Ruin

Upon Your Dreams They Prey: A Lullaby

Vanguard

Vida's Sixth Trip Around the Sun

When Sheds Talk

AND THE MOON IS FULL AND BRIGHT

ONE

Chef Andres Mosse was something of a legend.

Having come up as one of the (now infamous) Four Horsemen of Punk Cuisine, as they were known, he was without question the most elusive chef of the bunch.

Elusive in the sense that I needed to travel almost four thousand miles south from New York City—to a place so off-the-grid it lacked any formal name—just to ask him a single crucial question.

Would he appear on my fledgling television show?

Sitting inside a cramped thirty-six square foot hut that smelled of fresh dirt and bitter cassava, deep in the cool, mid-winter remote wilderness of the Andes Mountain range, I watched him prepare us tea using tools that could have existed thousands of years before.

Nobody could accuse Chef Andres Mosse of being *moderne*.

They never really could. Of all the Horsemen, he'd always been the greatest purveyor of rustic and traditional cooking methods.

That, along with his brusque style and showman's tendency for panache, made him among the first culinary stars to boil over into the public consciousness via the airwaves.

He was perhaps most infamous for his stunt at the Grand Prix, where he'd roasted every single part of a chicken—brain, liver, eggs, breast, feet, wings, and thighs—in an elevated and elaborate response to one of the judges who had previously called him a chicken for having bolted from the head chef position at Europe's most preeminent restaurants (at the time, as those things tend to change faster than the seasons) in favor of hanging his own shingle in a small roadside café near Leticia, Colombia.

His mastery was such that even the judges could not help but award him the prize.

Looking around the hut, I could see, at least, that his rustic style hadn't changed much.

I didn't see any evidence of chickens, though.

"So you'd like me to appear on your television show," he said, grabbing the towel slung over his shoulder to handle the hot teakettle.

"Not just appear," my producer, John Jacques, said, "Benjamin here and I want you to star."

I rolled my eyes, glad at least he didn't spread his hands across the space above his head like a cabaret dancer. John had a flair for the dramatic. I often wondered if he'd prefer to host the show rather than me. He'd probably be better.

"I'm flattered," Andres said, his exotic sounding accent having been flattened since his early days with the Horseman. I'd heard a rumor that he didn't even actually speak with one, that he'd developed it early on for his first show and it stuck.

One of many rumors about this man.

He poured the steaming water into three mismatched ceramic cups. Cups that looked like they could have been crafted by the ancient Indians who populated this area. Ancestors of the sherpas who'd guided us to Andres's cabin for the equivalent of four US dollars.

The bitter smell from the raw tea leaves gave way to a smooth and slightly sweet scent.

He turned his massive body, silhouetted against the falling afternoon sun streaming in through the window behind him, and held a tray with the cups of tea out so we could each take one.

He did not sit down.

"Flattered," he said again over the sudden barking of some wild animal I was unable to identify. "And I've always respected your work, Benjamin. Felt a sort of kinship, maybe, in that you never got comfortable doing some shtick. A few of my boys in the original crew cut themselves down at the knees, ya know."

I nodded. Probably talking about Lincoln and Uhls, two of his Horseman compatriots who morphed from talented chefs to television personalities, both hosting a bevy of long-running cooking competition shows that were nearly indistinguishable from one another. The lifestyle afforded them much—penthouse apartments, exclusive access to VIP events and parties, the sort of lives where the complaints became ones of want rather than lack. But it wasn't hard to notice—as someone who'd known the Horsemen in their early days —that Lincoln and Uhls now lacked the edge and mountain-sized chips on their shoulders that made them noteworthy in the first place. That was something Andres had never lost. Though compared to Andres's current digs, even Fred Flintstone looked posh.

"But unfortunately, I no longer do television. I apologize you both came all this way to find that out. And that you brought a crew, however skeleton," he leaned closer, "though I'm not entirely upset you brought the one."

He winked at me. Talking about Lucy, clearly.

"If only you'd phoned, I could have saved you the trouble."

For once, John sat there, open-mouthed. Smart enough not to insult (though Andres might actually have enjoyed that) but not quick enough to come up with a retort.

"I kid, of course," Andres said, gesturing around to the hut, which lacked even the most basic conveniences of life at the turn of the eighteenth century, let alone a phone line.

It would have been funny, I'm sure, had either John or I slept more than a few minutes in the past thirty-six hours. We had somehow, very stupidly, convinced ourselves that what this trip would lack in creature comforts and traditional twenty-first century travel methods—like airplanes larger than coffins and automobiles produced after the Vietnam War—we would more than make up for in historic residuals.

After skipping past the inevitable deal we'd strike for a television show at a major network.

Hell, if what we'd heard was true, maybe we'd even be simulcast.

John started to speak but I cut him off. No amount of theatrics was going to change Andres's mind.

Another tact would be necessary.

"Andres, this show is different than the others," I said, trying to project a confidence I didn't feel. "We're not out to produce a hoity-toity cooking show with all the glitz and glamor of a magazine photo shoot. We're after something ... grittier."

Andres sipped his steaming cup of tea but said nothing.

It was time to see if one particular rumor about Andres Mosse held any water. The one I'd practically had to pry from Danner Winston, a chef who owed me a big, Jupiter-sized favor and who I'd plied with more than a few of his favorite drinks until he was good and ready to spill his guts.

Danner had always been a guy with his finger on the pulse. Not a Horseman, but he was part of the same ilk. He was like the Tom Hagen of the culinary world—he saw everything.

If the rumor Danner told me was true, this trip would be worth it thirty times over.

If not, John and I could finish our tea and start the thirty-six-hour return trip now.

We'd have to find our pilot episode elsewhere.

"This world you're living in out here," I continued, "it's important. I think you know that. Now it's time to share it with the rest of the world."

Andres put a hand over the steaming cup and seemed to enjoy the warmth against his hand.

"*This world*," he said slowly, twisting up his nose, "I'm not sure I follow."

I took a sip from the tea and let the tart, warm liquid settle into my chest. It was strong and packed a double punch. Once in your throat and once in your belly. Different from anything I'd tasted back in New York.

And that's the tact I decided to use.

"You've lived where we've lived, more or less. If not always physically, then psycho-spiritually. You've seen the cities, the news, the culture. People are losing their edge and their spirit. *This*," I motioned all around us, "is pretty far off the beaten path."

He crossed his arms.

"The world at large is getting soft, Andres. You've returned to something much more primal. More real. Focused on the things that matter."

"Oh? And why must I share that with the world? Let them figure it out for themselves, if they choose to."

I put the cup down.

"What about ... the meals?"

A flicker of something behind his eyes. Brief, almost completely hidden behind his bearded, rugged facade.

But there all the same.

"The meals are what we're after, Andres," John said. I wished he hadn't. I could almost see Andres retreat away from the words.

Which was telling in and of itself.

Andres was a man of great pride and self-assurance. Had to have been to have been a Horseman. Anybody who lived through that era (think: Lower East Side, late '70s, smack practically in the water supply) was a mentally tough S.O.B. Probably more than a little crazy, too.

So if he winced at our mention of the meals, he still needed to be convinced they were kosher, so to speak.

"It's not simply the meals," I corrected John. "It's everything that comes with them. Doing it all yourself. No crews, no sous chefs. Not even any of that farm-to-table crap."

(I said this for effect. I'd owned a labor of love farm-to-table place only three years earlier.)

Andres shifted from one foot to the other.

"We want the original farm-to-table," John said. "Inca warrior style."

I smacked the table in front of John, making him spill some of his tea. He must have been really feeling the fatigue because he was spouting off all the ignorant stuff I'd told him not to say—the stuff that would make Andres shut down and send us packing.

Andres looked at me. I hoped he saw in me some sort of kindred spirit, though my bluster only went so far.

I lived in one of the biggest cities in the world and ate in restaurants.

He lived off the land in a place that hadn't been inhabited since the sixteenth century.

"I'm just not sure I can help you," he said.

"We want to come on the hunt with you," I said.

That got his attention.

"The hunt." He said the words out loud as if he were tasting them, swishing them around his palette like a fine wine.

"For the werewolves."

Saying it out loud scared me a little, to be honest. Prior to that moment, none of this had been totally real to me. Of course, I knew where this might be headed, if the rumors proved true (as unlikely as that seemed).

But now that the word *werewolves* was hanging in the air between us, I could not go back.

Andres cut his eyes between John and me. He gave us a wince that turned into a broad and devious smile. It reminded me of the famous cover of *Bon Appétit* he'd done after opening his first restaurant. A high-resolution, close-up, black-and-white photo of Andres, his face rugged, even then. It was a mug that had so much character, one could not help but be pulled in. When he was the talk of the culinary world.

The excited, next-big-thing talk, at least.

There was still plenty of talk of Andres.

But it was mostly scared whispers.

He started laughing, something vaguely Kurtzian that frankly scared the shit out of me.

"Good on you, boys," he said, draining his tea.

I'd barely touched mine. The first sip of it had given me a warm buzz like a strong whiskey.

Andres stood up. He seemed like he took up the entire room. I'd run into him a few times over the years, at random culinary events. On the now-trite food festivals and typical television promotional stuff.

He'd never seemed so big to me. So tough. Like John Colter of the Andes.

I wondered how much of it was due to his new life down here.

His new diet.

How much of that toughness might be required of me, were he to let us come with him?

"Just because you want to come doesn't mean you'll get what you're after. Out here, there are no guarantees."

"We understand," I said, though I wasn't sure that was true.

He sighed. Grimaced in a way that made me think he was going to say no, suddenly, a change of heart, shutting himself off without warning or explanation. I almost spoke up, cut him off, wanting to be sure that I didn't allow him to give us one more no before using my ace in the hole, should I need it.

But something held me back.

Then he spoke.

"Very well," he said to us both. "Your timing is good, I'll give you that. Get some rest. We leave tonight."

He walked out of the hut and turned black against the dying late afternoon sun.

In seconds he'd merged into the wild surrounding landscape like an Apache.

John turned to me and just raised an eyebrow. "I guess we're doing this," he said.

I was stunned stupid for a moment. Then a shiver of premonition washed over me.

We had landed our white whale.

This would be a huge event. Would put our show on the map. Launch us into the goddamned stratosphere.

We'd be the talk of not just the television cooking world.

We'd be the talk of the whole world, period.

For someone with no prior experience making a television show, this was akin to unwrapping a golden ticket in my Wonka bar.

I thought I'd feel relief. Or elation. Some wind under our sails.

But I didn't feel any of those things.

Instead, I felt only the imminent chill of night at the door.

TWO

Rest didn't come easy in the intervening hours after Andres agreed.

His camp had four other huts of similar size to the one we'd had tea in. That one appeared to also be the closest thing to a kitchen, with a fire pit out back sheltered from the elements by the same rusted corrugated metal roofing that covered everything else.

One hut was Andres's, and none of us dared go near it after he went inside with a stunning brunette woman who had emerged from an opening in the tree line the same way Andres had disappeared into it earlier.

We weren't that close geographically (but we *were* in the neighborhood), so I nicknamed her the Amazon.

From the moment I saw her, I couldn't get her out of my mind. She was simply there one moment when the moment before she was not. Her skin was mocha, her body both angular and curved in all the right places.

And her eyes. They had stared out at us, knowingly, as if she knew we would be here.

Not a single second of surprise.

Almost two hours later, as the golden sun descended into a

purple specter floating through the thick foliage around us, they still hadn't emerged.

I'd never been so jealous of a man in my entire life.

Two of the other huts were used to store equipment like shovels, a few wheelbarrows, scythes. There were old fiberglass bows and wooden arrows tucked into quivers that were long past their prime. All arranged neatly along the walls next to newer rifles and a single shotgun.

Quite a lot of weaponry for a single man to require.

The last hut was where our crew posted up. Furnished with two chairs and two hammocks, it was probably better accommodations than could be found anywhere in a hundred square miles.

But it was far from the Ritz.

Nate, our cameraman, had taken one of the hammocks at my insistence. John lay in the other one, half-asleep.

I'd insisted that Lucy, our sound technician, take that one, but she took one look at John and sat in the chair across from me.

Apparently John had been too tired to resist the first bed-like thing we'd seen in the past day-and-a-half.

Both Nate and Lucy were younger than John and me. Late twenties and they looked it.

Nate was a former college wide receiver and still carried himself like it—in a good way. He seemed to be dealing with the physicality of this particular project alright (that is to say, better than either of his elder statesman), though right now he was sacked up like a freshman trying to catch a few winks of sleep during two-a-days.

Lucy, too, seemed to be holding up. She wasn't quite the cheerleader to Nate's receiver, though she certainly had the looks for it. Instead she'd done track—javelin and pole vault—at a small Division III college in Arizona because, as she'd put it, tongue firmly in cheek, "I was more interested in parties than poles."

John had looked her up when she agreed to work with us and found a bevy of New York State high school records in both events littering some old high school webpage.

She was a beautiful blonde with long, toned legs and an equally toned ... everything else. Proving the old adage that female pole vaulters have the best bodies in all of athletics.

God bless them.

I hadn't any hand in hiring her, though if I had, I wouldn't have hesitated. Beauty, sure, but she'd proven to be plenty resourceful on our long journey down to the Andes. Especially in some of the sketchier traverses where we passed through dangerous jungle checkpoints and negotiated with gruff fisherman to ride us across rivers as desolate as the surface of the moon.

Besides, a true mark of someone was whether or not you could take a road trip with them. And we'd just taken the road trip from hell and had yet to be at each other's throats.

"How's the equipment?" I asked Lucy, keeping my voice down so as not to wake the others.

She nodded, pulling a sweatshirt made of a heavy technical cotton out of her pack. "Checks out. There wasn't much here to begin with. And what we've got is built to take a beating."

"Once we get the show up and running, I promise you the best shotgun mic money can buy."

She smiled, pulling her sweatshirt on. "This stuff will do fine."

I forgot how being young can do a lot to dampen expectations. She wasn't far from being out of college, working in her first job in television, and was hungry to make a name for herself.

I could relate. And I felt a responsibility to her and Nate to make this show the best it could be.

We'd gotten seed money to shoot this pilot from a small production company where John had a connection. Based on the amount of seed money, they weren't confident in our success. As it was, we were tied together with shoestrings and good luck (we could easily be stuck in out-of-the-way places in four different countries right now).

If any of us had been a financial advisor, the prevailing thought would have been *not* to invest what little money we had on such an unlikely option.

I guess we had more of a tolerance for risk.

And the bombed-out road of my past was littered with risky bets that blew up in my face.

Maybe one day I'd learn to play it safe.

The door to Andres's cabin opened up behind me. I turned back to see the Amazon step out into the broken light the color of pomegranate seeds. Her eyes caught mine and I felt my throat catch and a few other things tighten. She might have been the most beautiful woman I'd ever seen. And I was sitting only a few feet away from a woman who turned every head from New York to depths of the Andes.

Part of me wondered if the whole werewolf thing was a complete charade, something Andres went with in the moment to put us on. I felt confident my source had heard the rumor. Even felt confident *he* believed it.

But now that I saw the Amazon, I wondered if Andres had found this immaculate woman somehow and decided to hell with the rest of the world. Who could blame him if he had? Certainly not me. If she walked over here and asked me to do the same, I'd walk right off into the dark jungle and let her lead me to a pygmy army of hungry cannibals.

Andres emerged behind the Amazon with a worried look on his face. Not exactly what I was expecting. But when you let a woman as incredible looking as her walk out of your bedroom, there had to be some innate dread deep inside you that said you might never see her walk back in.

"Is this the part where we get the safety briefing?" Lucy whispered to me. "Keep hands and feet inside the vehicle at all times?"

I glanced at Lucy and shrugged.

When I looked back, the Amazon was gone.

Andres walked toward us, flicking on a flashlight to combat what was very suddenly almost total darkness. Only a dying flicker of dark purple was still visible on the edge of the mountains far beyond where we stood.

Looking at him, I got that same shiver from earlier. As the sun dropped, so too did the temperature. I followed Lucy's lead and pulled out my own sweatshirt. We'd all brought as many different layers as we could fit, unsure of what kind of weather or conditions would await us down here.

"Rested?" Andres asked, standing outside our door.

I wasn't. Lucy seemed fine. Nate and John were still out cold in the hammocks.

I guess three out of four rested would have to do.

"Benjamin, why don't you help me load everything up?" he said, starting back toward the huts where we'd seen the equipment.

"How long 'til we leave?" I asked.

"Just getting dark now," Andres said over his shoulder. "We'll hike in thirty minutes."

"How long are we going for?" Lucy asked.

Andres turned, gave her a long look. "As long as it takes, my lady. But at least two days, I'd say. We hike tonight, hunt tomorrow night." Then he turned again and walked away.

"Wake these guys up," I said to Lucy, closing my pack up.

"You need any help, you think?"

I looked out after Andres, his calm, committed walk through the dark clearing sending a wave of uncertainty over me.

This all suddenly seemed very real. We were no longer in the confines of New York City. Or America. Or any damn place where rules applied.

As the last of the light dropped over the horizon and the nocturnal song of the jungle crawled from its hiding spot, I realized how truly and utterly alone we were out here.

I said none of this, though.

Instead, I simply said, "Nope. Just make sure these boys got their beauty sleep."

Then I walked out of the hut and followed Andres into the darkness.

THREE

We hiked a few kilometers up a treacherous, switch-backed route through hardly touched wilderness. The air was refreshing at first, only punctuated by the occasional stench of rotting wood or an unseen animal carcass. But as we kept on, it grew thinner, the hike more arduous.

Andres took the lead, his massive form and swift machete making it so John and I could follow closely behind. Lucy and Nate pulled up the rear.

The pathway up took us through dense forest. Thick enough to get tangled up in, pulled deeper, suffocated without a sound.

Only the last few hundred yards of murderous uphill climbing had it thinned. Now we could start to see cracks in the vegetation, a few shadowed lumps besides the two feet of pitch black on either side of us.

We'd been forced by circumstance to travel light.

Behind us, Nate and Lucy had started by testing out their gear again as we went, making sure that if we actually found ourselves killing and then eating a werewolf, the rest of the world could see it. We'd do it *"Blair Witch* style," as Nate was so fond of saying, even making us watch the movie on the Devil's Nose train—a scenic marvel through Ecuador that could not be less suited to hunching over an old laptop watching a black-and-white found footage film. After about twenty minutes, I'd had to close my eyes to prevent myself from puking, the camera movements were so jerky in conjunction with the moving train.

I certainly hoped our show didn't have the same effect.

After the first twenty minutes on the trail, both Nate and Lucy had fallen quiet, their breathing the only evidence of their presence behind me.

The push up to wherever we were headed took all precedence and energy.

So far we hadn't seen anything, though Andres told us that would be the case. He didn't live near the werewolf den for obvious reasons.

"If I had," he said when I asked him, "you'd have never tracked me down. Not without a few forensic anthropologists anyway."

"Not a gravedigger, too?" I asked, trying to make a joke.

"The civilized dig graves, Benjamin. There's nothing civilized about where we're headed."

Not exactly comforting.

"Besides, there wouldn't be enough of me left for a burial."

We came to a clearing that appeared almost instantly after scrambling up a tree-lined narrow finger of a path covered in loose stones. It was cut through a massive boulder, the hulking rock walls on either side of us seeming to close in as we got closer to the top.

I was breathing hard from the hike and the elevation.

Hard enough to not be able to hear if anybody else was behind me. We'd had no time to acclimatize, which worried me. I wasn't sure how much farther we had to go.

Looking around the clearing, though, it didn't seem we'd be going any higher up.

The only thing above us was the moon, tamped down by thick grey clouds.

But the view was astounding.

It was possible some of my inability to breathe as we climbed was due to us hiking through clouds.

We were that high.

I cut a glance at Andres, who was watching our group with an unreadable expression cast in long shadows. Draped in darkness. Only the glint of his eyes was visible against the dull silver hue of the smoky moonlight.

Below us, a massive bowl of a valley sat stoic and still. It seemed to stretch on forever. Just like Andres, it sat in varying shades of inky shadows cast by the odd glow of the moon. Estuaries of vegetation trickled down different parts of the mountains, stopping and starting as if by some unseen hand. Peaks and crags hung against the grey night sky like mangled fingers.

Even just the outline of the moon through the clouds looked enormous. Being several thousand feet higher than Manhattan—not to mention without any of the bright lights of the city—really makes a difference, apparently. Part of me felt like we could reach out and pull ourselves up to the heavens.

Andres handed me a canteen of water. "One of the strangest places on earth as far as lunar activity."

"Is that why they're concentrated here?" John asked.

Andres nodded. "Some of the rumors you've heard are true. The moonlight plays a contributing factor in their life cycle, though of course we have no real idea why. It brings the beasts out of their shell, so-to-speak.

"And because the moon is so clear and high in the sky here, especially right now, they can exist in their changed state for longer now than most other places on earth. And tomorrow we'll see the Wolf Moon."

Lucy and I looked at each other.

"Wolf Moon?" John said, setting his pack on the ground.

Andres pulled something from his own pack and fiddled with it silently in the darkness. "The Wolf Moon is the first full moon of the year. Traditionally named, for centuries, by both European and

Native American peoples in the Northern Hemisphere. A lot of rituals and superstitions revolved around it. Simply put, though, wolves tended to howl most in January. So the name stuck."

"But the seasons are reversed here," I said, my mind trying to keep up but struggling with the lack of oxygen. My heart was still pounding and my skull felt tight around my brain.

Now that we were up here, most of my doubts about Andres had fallen away. If he had been pulling a prank on us, it was an elaborate one. And one he must have pulled before, given how little he'd hesitated so far on our journey.

But after seeing the Amazon, I couldn't help but be at least a little skeptical. I could see how a man like Andres could be pulled toward the allure this place, that were wasn't a single thing else he needed in the world that wasn't already here.

I tried to put all that out of my mind, though. We'd always have time to fact check and edit later.

"That they are, Benjamin. I see you've done the bare minimum of research required when traveling halfway around the world." He grinned. "I imported the name. Once I made the discovery of the werewolves. Seems awfully fitting here, given the effect it has."

He had a point there.

"Are you the first person to have found these things?" I asked, taking up the mantle as television show host. "I would think word of such a thing would make the news. Be known worldwide."

Andres shook his head no. "Not the first. But one of the few still alive."

I shuddered. "And this ... Wolf Moon ..."

"Yes, my own name for it. But the name fits like a glove, old boy. Don't you worry. Do you have a guess as to why?"

I didn't. Not even a clue.

"Really?" Andres said. He looked around at John and Nate. And one longer glance at Lucy.

None of them had any clue, either.

If I ever got to make another episode of television in my life, I'd be sure to hire a damned researcher for any and all trips. Our production company hadn't thought us a solid enough investment to fund that.

Andres laughed, a devious mortar shell of a laugh. He doubled over, unable to contain himself.

I didn't get the joke.

Which in my experience meant the joke was on me.

"Oh lord, you all *slay* me. A bunch of rag-taggers, you are. If I'd any question before about whether your little television show would take off, well I've none now."

"What's that supposed to mean?" John said, stepping toward Andres in much too aggressive of a way for anybody to take seriously.

Which just sent Andres into a bigger fit of laughter. Just to show you how scared he was at the prospect of fighting John.

"It wasn't an insult, man. In my experience in television, there's one main skill you need."

"And what's that?" I said.

"You need to be like a cat. Always land with your feet on the ground."

"What does that mean?" Lucy said.

"You need to be luckier than an English royal."

Still nothing. I didn't have the faintest idea about what he was talking about.

Which only made Andres laugh again, clapping his hands. "Oh mates. Everything you do needs to come up roses."

"Can you translate that, Andres?"

"You lot have really stepped in it," he said, wiping the back of a beefy hand against his cheek, wet from tears. "I mean, almost no amount of planning whatsoever could have put you in such a perfect spot. And none of you even knows it!"

I saw John looking at me. Confused. And maybe a little scared.

"Tomorrow night is the winter solstice, mates. Longest night of the year."

A shiver of terrified sweat dripped down my spine.

"Prime night to find us some werewolves."

FOUR

Andres let us rest in the clearing while he went off somewhere out of sight.

He assured me that we were in no danger here. Which didn't stop me from sweating despite the damp chill in the air.

I was simply too tired to stop him from going. And was happy for the rest.

Before Andres left, my head ached with a mixture of a vice grip and a pulsating knockout punch. My muscles not only ached but felt dry, like they were being aged in the meat locker at Gallaghers.

I pulled out my canteen and sipped more water than I felt comfortable drinking. But I'd been told once that hydration is the best way to combat the effects of altitude.

I guess everyone was tired because they were all doing the same thing.

A slow breeze pushed its way up the mountain from the direction we'd climbed. With it, a light fog rolled in, illuminated in a strange, silvery glow from the moon.

I don't know how long I sat like that but after a few moments, I could only make out the shapes of John, Lucy, and Nate. There was the occasional rustle to convince me they hadn't gone anywhere. I'm not sure what I would have done if they had.

The sound of them at least told me that I wasn't alone.

But my mind must have felt alone. Because I drifted slowly on the heels of the fog. Back to my conversation with Andres before we left camp.

He'd pried open the side door of one of the huts, revealing a closet full of beautiful, shimmering metallic weapons hung from small pegs on the wall. The flashlight danced across them as Andres took them in.

There were blades—short and long, serrated and smooth. Hilts made of worn leather, each with a sharp point sticking out from the bottom. Curved blades, too. A scythe head, missing its handle. A few things that looked vaguely Eastern in origin, though I would be the last person able to say which culture they came from exactly.

Next to those was a two-headed axe, its handle almost three feet long. It looked heavy, seemed to strain the pegs beneath it.

"All silver," he said, nodded at the weapons. "Heavier than shit, they are."

My eyes continued on as Andres moved his light to illuminate additional items.

The next thing was a strange looking item I'd never seen before. It was two pieces, connected to one another by a thick chain. One piece looked almost like a crescent moon. The other looked at first like a lightning bolt. As I got closer, it looked, bizarrely, more dangerous than one.

"A Wolfsangel," Andres said, noticing where my gaze had stopped.

"What is it?"

"Like most things, that all depends on who's looking at it."

I stepped closer, strangely enthralled by the instrument. Andres shined the flashlight to it.

The larger of the two pieces had dull edges. Probably meant to be held. The smaller piece looked to be the dangerous one. Its steel was sharp on all edges. It had clearly been used plenty. Chinks in the armor, so to speak. Nothing to indicate any of that use had damaged the thick steel structure.

But whatever this was, it held its own.

"This beauty right here originated in Germany. Based on ancient wolf traps. The curved part is hung from a tree. Bait is strung around this part here." He pointed to the lightning bolt shaped part. "The wolf chomps down and *whap*," Andres placed a hooked finger in his cheek and yanked.

"That's ... horrible," I said, wondering if that was hypocritical or not.

He waved his hand. "Old times. Embellished tales, I'm sure."

"Oh? And why do you have one, then?"

"Historically, this thing was used more for its symbol than its utility. It became a prominent symbol in boatloads of heraldic charges of the great Saxon dynasties of old, all the way up through the twentieth century."

"What happened then?"

Andres raised an eyebrow. "Look at that thing. It's a German symbol of power and distinction. What do you think happened to it?"

I nodded, a bit embarrassed by my question.

Andres clapped me on my back. "Get the silly questions out now. Better than when you're on camera, eh? Anyway, you're all hung up on the old stuff. It's a new day, mate. We use these now."

He flipped open a wooden box set off to the right of the other weapons. Inside were loads of silver bullets, stacked pristinely and in perfect order. They gleamed under the flashlight's glow.

"Would be a hell of a time to take down one of those bastards with anything but these."

Andres pulled the entire box out from its shelving and put the flashlight between his teeth. After taking a long look at the bullets, he pulled out at least a dozen and rolled them along in the palm of his massive hand.

Apparently satisfied, he slipped the bullets into his coat pocket and put the box back.

"Who was the woman?" I asked.

He hardly missed a beat. "What woman?" He reached past me into the closet and took two knives—one short and one long. The short one he placed into a small scabbard hooked to his belt on the right side. The long one went into a scabbard that hung down near his left leg.

"Andres."

He sighed. "Oh, you mean Quille." He said this as if we'd been walking in a crowded city square surrounded by women. Though, after seeing Quille, as he called the Amazon, I suppose maybe Andres actually was.

Quille. An odd name. Sounded smooth coming from his mouth. It would not have from mine.

"Right. Who is she?"

"Would you like anything from the armory?" he asked me.

I just glared at him. I didn't have the faintest idea what I would do with any of it.

He started to close the door. I put my hand on his arm to stop him.

"I'll take something," I said, opting for a short knife that at least looked like I wouldn't hurt myself with. He handed me a worn leather sheath with a metal clip that I slid onto my belt.

We were going after werewolves, after all.

"You should put that at your back," he said with a smirk. "Less likely to get caught on things. Strap your pack so it sits above it."

"So who is she?" I asked him, trying not to let him deflect my questions.

He closed the door to the hut. "I believe you've reached your quota of silly questions, Benjamin."

"Andres, c'mon. You disappear for hours with a woman. You think we're not all curious?"

"You showed up at *my* doorstep. I would have thought moving here made it quite clear. I'm not open to visitors."

"You're a hermit now?"

"My business is my own."

And you've ruined it. He didn't speak the words, but I got his message.

"I'm sorry to barge in like this."

He rolled his eyes.

"You could have sent us away."

He stopped and looked me dead in the eyes. Behind them sat something wild and fierce that made me think twice about embarking on a journey into the wilderness with this man.

"You are here to film a television show, are you not?"

I nodded.

"And you are being graciously hosted to do so, are you not?"

I nodded again.

"Then a piece of advice. Graciously accept what is given to you. You have not forgotten about Frankfurt, have you? Eh?"

My face reddened, gave way to what I'm sure was an expression of subjugation. Though I should not have been surprised.

Frankfurt had been on my mind since before we even started the trip. It was the only reason why I'd jumped at the opportunity to convince Andres Mosse—an old acquaintance, if not a friend—to allow us to film him doing something that no one had ever captured on film before.

It had been the perfect opportunity for our show to skip the proverbial line in the television world. To make our own luck.

It was the reason I took four hundred of our seed money to visit Danner Winston and lube him up with fifty-dollar rounds of twenty-plus year single malt scotch in a greasy dumpling joint (his favorite) in Chinatown, to get him to open up about where Andres was these days.

Because we'd been through something together. Something that, God willing, no one else would ever know about.

I'd just as soon as him not bring it up.

"You thought I'd forgotten about Frankfurt?" he said with an unreadable expression on his face. Did he think this was funny? Was he taking pity?

"I ... no, I just ..."

Andres clapped a meaty hand on my back. "Say no more about it, mate. Just make sure you're ready to go in twenty."

I said no more about it. What else was there to say? Instead, I just stood motionless watching Andres walk back toward his cabin to make whatever other preparations he needed to make.

FIVE

Now I watched Andres emerge from the thick fog that had gathered, his shadowy face hidden from view until he was practically right on top of me.

I snapped out of my reverie and took another long gulp of water. It tasted good. Clean and fresh. I realized I'd stopped sweating. And my head, while not exactly clear, no longer was too excruciating for me to think.

Andres reached his hand out and helped me back to my feet. A bit unsteady. But capable of continuing.

"You alright, mate?"

I nodded. "The rest did me well."

The wind picked up, came rushing over the boulders we'd trekked through to make it into the clearing. It dissipated some of the fog just enough so the forms of John, Lucy, and Nate were once again visible.

I was relieved that all three of them looked better than I felt. More chipper. Nate and Lucy were even stretching a bit to stay loose in the chill.

Andres reached into his bag and opened up his hand.

"Jerky," he said. "You lot haven't had anything to eat since you got here."

"Is it ... ?" I asked, turning over the dry meat.

"No. Haven't tried to do jerky with it yet. Not a bad idea, though."

"We could do it for this episode," I offered, taking a bite of the jerky.

"No," John said, coming closer. "Bonus content, maybe, but not for the episode."

He was right, of course.

Given the risks we'd taken to come here, it made no sense to waste that opportunity making jerky with a world-class chef. Like I said, John was the dramatic one. Had an eye for this sort of thing.

And he was right. Of all the culinary delights a chef of Andres Mosse's caliber could prepare, not a single one had less sizzle than jerky.

It would be like asking the Rolling Stones to play *Mary Had a Little Lamb* on tambourine.

Though, of course, if we captured footage of us killing a werewolf, we could make whatever we damn well pleased and it wouldn't make a wink of difference.

"Right, well this will be our last real rest. After this, we move to the staging area. Should be safe there, relatively. During the day will be fine. But make no mistake, over this ridge here? It's all the war zone."

For the second time that night, the gravity of what we were about to do hit me. This was insanity. Both that it was happening and that we were doing it. And doing it on film that we were going to use to secure us a television show.

Maybe what Andres had said was right.

Better to be lucky than good.

I motioned Nate and Lucy up to us and handed them each some jerky. It was perfectly cooked, not tough at all. There was a hint of sweetness to it—honey was my guess—and a healthy dusting of cayenne. Delicious, whatever it was.

I handed the rest of it to John.

All of us ate it. Hungry travelers, chewing in silence.

That was the first time I noticed it. The quiet. It was as if we'd ascended so high above everything else that all noise besides the wind had ceased. There were no animals. No little critters skittering around. No broken sticks.

It was strange. Slightly disturbing. Even more so coming from New York.

"Here is dessert," Andres said. He pulled a cloth bag the size of a reporter's notebook from his jacket pocket. It was full of something, almost packed to the gills.

He handed it to me first.

"Take a handful, pass it along," he said.

I did. Opened my hand to find a dozen tiny purple berries. Smaller than blueberries, even, but juicy and plump, as if they were bursting with inner life.

"What are these?" I poked one of them with my finger, getting its purple juice on the tip.

"Lycanberries. Native to this region, for a very special reason."

"What reason is that?" John asked, pressing his face close to his palm to take a smell of them.

"They are the closest thing to an antidote to werewolves that exist."

I looked over and was relieved to find Nate already getting this footage on tape. Lucy was right next to him, making sure the audio feed was working well on our lapel mics before picking up the cheap boom mic we'd managed to pay for and bring along.

Time to start working, I guess.

I moved in front of the camera and let Nate get a close-up shot of the berries.

This was some guerilla footage, that was for sure.

"Can you explain that?"

Andres did. Apparently the berries had a certain level of acidity to them that reacted with the human blood. Rare to find in anything edible. A handful of them would mask the blood in your body. Change its taste.

"And that is the only thing that will save you if a werewolf gets a hold of you."

"Why is that?" I asked.

"They hate the taste. They'll take a bite, sure. But, similar to how a shark bites into a surfer and lets go because sharks prefer seal meat to humans, this stuff in your blood will make it so werewolves move on to greener pastures. Let you alone."

I looked at the berries again. "But it only works once they bite you?"

"Or any other way they could get a taste of your blood. But yeah."

"That's not exactly comforting," I said.

"Have any of you ever been hunting before?" Andres asked. He was a veteran of television and so had to have known he was breaking the illusion of what we were creating. Not that I cared much. It was just the five of us out here. Part of the reason John and I wanted to make this show was to get away from the over-produced crap that made up so much of TV today. We wanted something more like real life.

Adventures in Heightened Reality was our original concept. I'll take credit for that one.

Nate raised his hand to answer Andres's question.

"Then it bears mentioning for the rest of you. This isn't some theme park ride. Injuries can happen—even before we get into the mix with the werewolves. Just because it doesn't seem fair to you that a mudslide takes out half the mountain when we're on it? Doesn't mean it won't happen.

"You didn't want to get attacked and eaten by a werewolf? Well, it can happen, so you need to do everything in your power to make sure it doesn't.

"Because once you're dead, that's the end of the story. No do-overs. Maybe the angels will listen to your sanctimonious blather. But in the meantime? Pay attention and be extra vigilant about safety."

His words scared me, as I'm sure they were intended to. I put my free hand in my pocket to shield it from the cold wind, which had picked up steadily ever since Andres came back.

"Out here there are no guarantees, right?" I said.

He nodded. "Now you're starting to get it, Benjamin."

I wasn't sure how true that was, but I didn't say anything.

"So what are you all waiting for?" he asked, looking around. "You going to eat your dessert or what?"

Like obedient servants, we all did. I ate two of the lycanberries first, which was probably a mistake. They were so tart they made my tongue curl up almost to the back of my throat.

Andres laughed. "Bitter beer face, all of you. I never said it was pleasant."

He seemed to be enjoying himself. Which I hoped would at least make for good TV.

I slammed back the rest of the berries, trying to chew them as little as possible. And then we were done.

"Andres," I said, trying to collect my thoughts, "before we get started, I have a few questions."

He nodded.

I went to stand next to him so Nate could more easily film our discussion.

John made a motion to his own mouth once we got set up and Nate confirmed he was getting good enough light. Indicating I needed to wipe mine.

"Lycanberry juice," Andres laughed, clapping me on the back. Teasing me. "I remember my first werewolf hunt."

That was as good an opening as any.

"First of all, what is it like to eat them?"

"It's game meat on steroids, mate. The good kind of steroids—the ones that make your vision sharper and pumps up not only your body but your mind, too. Not to mention what it does for your pecker."

Everybody laughed at that, even me.

"We can edit that out," John said.

"You can edit out gold all day, mate," Andres said. "But don't forget I had the hottest cooking show on the planet back before it was even a thing."

Andres had that. His show was part punk-rock talk show, part experiential journalism. Some part of me probably used it as a touchstone when thinking of this show.

"Alright, alright," I said, trying to regain control. "Tell us about how you got started doing this? How did you get involved with werewolves?"

A flicker of something danced behind his eyes. Pain? Anger? Maybe the sort of pity only possible when asked a question that belied a deep misunderstanding of a subject?

Whatever it was, the mood suddenly changed, grew darker.

"Don't go all cold on us now," I said, trying to lighten it back up. "Tell us about it."

So he did.

Andres hadn't come to South America to find werewolves. Hadn't even known they existed, actually.

Instead, he came on a quest of sorts.

"Things back home," he said, shaking his head and looking off into the distance, "they'd kind of stopped making sense to me."

"How so?"

At this he looked at me with something akin to pure hatred. It was gone in an instant but unmistakably there. In that moment, I knew what he was talking about.

"I guess my current self at the time needed to escape his past. Mostly, I just needed to get away."

I was suddenly awash in a foggy memory which I tried to bat away, back into the murky depths of my subconscious by keeping the conversation going. And, like I'd been doing for so long, pretending as if nothing had actually happened.

"You've always been on the forefront of culinary trends. Maybe even ahead of the curve."

He nodded and continued talking, apparently happy to move past the old memory I'd somehow stumbled upon.

He'd always been an iconoclast, someone not afraid to buck the traditional system and hoe his own road. But even in so doing, he found that his mind needed to be expanded.

"No matter how hard I pushed, I was still knocking up against the gutters."

"What do you mean by that?" I asked him.

"When you're immersed in a culture—no matter who you are—you find it difficult to imagine the edges. What seems like radical thought is, in fact, only a standard deviation or two away from the middle. It's why the Free Love movement eventually lost steam. You get a group of people to veer off and out on the edges of—and this is the important part—*mainstream thought*, and that changes things. But there's always a regression back to the middle. And you can't make two leaps of the same size and intensity. Not with any sort of critical mass, anyway.

"People simply can't handle that sort of thing. And so any real radical change dies on the vine."

I was of two minds here. One was that Andres was coming off as an eloquent, if not esoteric, guest right now.

The other was that he was espousing radical theory on my damn TV show.

Which, I supposed, was exactly what John and I were after. So I pushed him farther.

"And so you came here seeking ... what exactly?"

"What everyone else is seeking. Enlightenment."

He'd traveled deep into the Amazon first, near the border of Brazil and Colombia. There he found a traditional healer, a man who administered spiritual ayahuasca ceremonies using methods that existed before the Spanish came to conquer so much of the continent.

"It sounds cliché now, since so many wealthy people do it as a bucket list item. Co-opted. Like yoga. But back then, it wasn't a known quantity. That was what I liked about it. I don't need to go into the laborious details of everything it unlocked for me. But he helped me shed some serious baggage. I stayed with that healer for a long time. Months."

"You did ayahuasca for months?" Suddenly concerned we were being duped by a burned-out hippie instead of the man I'd known back in Civilization (as I was now thinking of it).

He shook his head. "I did it during ceremonies over the course of that time period. But it wasn't constant. Once or twice a week, probably. The rest of the time I spent cooking, exploring the wilderness. It helped me reconnect with the things I'd loved as a child. The things that I felt made me a good human being.

"Those were the things I'd lost during my *ascent*, as it were, in the culinary world. Those are the things everybody loses if they're not careful."

I nodded.

"But before my final ayahuasca ceremony, my healer came to me with the dosage and told me that it was time I went off on my own.

"'What you are seeking, you can only find alone,' he said to me. That night, I went deep into the jungle. Deeper than I'd ever gone before. Completely alone. And I guess I never really came back."

The raw emotion in Andres's voice was astounding. It tugged at my own throat and I saw John wipe at his face with the sleeve of his jacket.

This was a heavy, heavy moment.

"What did you find there?" I finally asked.

Andres thought about this for a long time. The wind continued to blow against us, its temperament growing increasingly frustrated. What had once been a breeze was growing into something much more menacing.

When he finally spoke up, Andres had some of the quiet rage I'd seen in him earlier at his makeshift armory.

"It sounds crazy, but I found peace. I had a vision of a single forgotten place on this planet where nature had twisted in on itself. A vicious place that would test me, push me to limits that hardly a soul on earth knew of."

Andres's voice was steady as he wiped his mouth with the sleeve of his jacket.

"And I learned something important during my quest to rediscover that place."

"What was that?" I said, wondering if I truly wanted the answer.

"Violent environments change a man."

SIX

Nate put his camera down for a moment when it was clear that the interview segment was over.

I took a deep breath, trying to let some of the tension out of my body. Andres's words carried a haunting weight to them that knotted me up inside. And, strangely, they'd struck a chord within me.

"Andres," Lucy said, puncturing the quiet, "what are we walking into here?"

Andres turned to her. The way he stood—between Lucy and me —he simply eclipsed her from my view.

"As you've all seen already, this is wild, rugged country. We exerted ourselves a good deal to climb this peak. Obviously, there's nowhere else for us to go but down."

He pointed to a copse of small trees and bushes at the other end of the clearing from the way we came.

"We'll be going that way. Back down the peak, into Werewolf Valley, as I like to call it. That's where they live, where they hunt. Luckily for us, and probably for the rest of the world, they are confined there. Once the sun comes up, they transform away from werewolves and back into their alternate forms."

A shiver ran down my spine. *Alternate forms.* It sounded like something out of a Hitler Youth brochure. And made me wonder about the ethics of all this. Though I had a hunch that Aristotle never wrote any treatises about werewolves.

"Once in the valley, it will be crucial that we stay together. These buggers are vicious hunters, so we must be equally vicious."

"Are they big?" John asked. He'd removed his jones cap from his head and the steam danced like a snake being charmed out of his hair before being whisked away by the wind. His jaw was clenched.

Andres turned toward him. "Massive. Like cape buffalo standing on two feet. But don't be fooled by their size, mate. They're not just brawlers. Sure, they'll get in a knock-down-drag-out with the best of them. Happy to. But they'll just as soon use their vile trickery to isolate and separate us.

"To them, it's just their nature. They kill for sport."

"Not to eat?" I said.

Andres shrugged. "They're only werewolves temporarily. A night at most. Their sustenance is chaos and slaughter. But without the lycanberries, they'll gnaw at you longer than you'd be comfortable with. And that's it for you."

None of us saying anything.

Andres adds, "The berries at least give you a chance. A bite or scratch from one of these bastards is like a venomous snake bite. Left untreated, it will kill you and turn you into one of them. But eating another handful of berries immediately following will give you a chance to stay human."

I clenched my fists to keep them from shaking. I saw Lucy again, Andres having turned to face John. Her face was an unreadable mask, though she gave me a nod and pointed to the sound equipment to let me know we were still recording.

I was so scared that I'd totally forgotten.

"The sound especially will be something to marvel at." He gave a long sideways glance at Lucy. "So pay attention and stay alert."

The wind was moaning now, a guttural, heinous sound that came up the side of the mountain and laid into all of us. Under different circumstances, it might have been scary, nature showing off its brute strength against us mere mortals.

But I had a feeling we'd be seeing enough of nature's wrath here soon.

Alternate forms. Those two words came crawling back to me. They marked the first time in this journey that I'd realized the true darkness behind what we'd signed up to do.

It seemed ... criminal. To kill an animal was one thing. But to kill one that was also a man when the sun came up?

That was something far worse.

Yet I said nothing. What did that say about me?

"We'll continue this way," Andres said, motioning toward the space he'd indicated would take us down into the valley. It sloped gently away from us and then disappeared into the night. Presumably because the slope went from gentle to death-defying.

Rugged country indeed.

"Andres," I said, the words jumping from my mouth like they were trying to escape a high-rise fire.

Nate and Lucy both looked up at me. Neither seemed particularly terrified about what we were about to do, which made me wonder if I was the outlier in this group or if they were simply too young to truly understand consequences yet.

I knew John had reservations about this. And he was a real mensch for coming anyway.

Could it be that Lucy and Nate were so focused on their ambitions to break into the television world that they weren't seeing the same issues with what we were about to do?

Or maybe they just thought werewolves were a fairy tale.

And what did I believe?

The farther we got into this, the less I was sure. Mainly because I knew Andres. Knew that he was many things, but a liar wasn't one of them. Had hunting and eating werewolves been a rumor he wanted to perpetuate, he could have done so by simply sending us on our way with a vague and mysterious *no*.

Instead, he wanted to show us the goods.

"Yes?" he said.

"Before we go, one last question." The words were out of my mouth before I truly realized I was speaking them.

I cut my eyes at John, expecting him to cut me off. "Action, action, action with a side of *action*," I'm pretty sure were his exact words when we discussed a strategy for coming here. "That's the key to making this show a success."

I'd said that we were after a cultured audience. The sort of people who watched television with some brains behind it. We didn't just want to do another trumped up competition show. We were after something *deeper*.

And that's the same reason we didn't have hardly any seed money.

"Only after we've established an audience," John said, would we be free to take chances and build out all the things we'd dreamed of.

I didn't necessarily agree. Besides, there was always the editing room to spruce up the footage Nate collected.

But John had insisted. "He takes us in, he shoots a werewolf, we watch this culinary master elevate his craft on an ingredient the world has never seen before. Period. Stop. End of story. Then we shop it around and decide if we want Fox's corporate suite at the World Series or the CBS box at the Super Bowl."

That was his recipe for success.

Now, though, he hardly seemed to hear what I said at all.

So I took that as a sign to press on.

Couldn't help myself.

"Why are you doing this?" I asked. "I mean, surely you know once the secret gets out, people will try to find this place. Why agree to let us come with you?"

Apparently taken aback by the question, Andres didn't have the answer on his tongue.

Once again, the wind bellowed up and over the edge of the clearing and punctuated the silence that hung between us for what felt like forever.

"We've known each other how long, Benjamin?"

I shrugged. "Long time. Fifteen years?"

He nodded. "Might be I'm getting nostalgic as I get older. Always good to see old friends."

I didn't say anything.

"Maybe it's because I don't think a single soul in this world will come here. They'll just make another Hot Pocket in the confines of their safe, air locked, temperature-controlled box they call a home, turn the channel, and argue about whatever the outrage of the day is."

Which very well could be true.

"Might just be that I owe you one, ya know?" he said, a wider, wolfish grin spreading across his face.

Lucy squinted her eyes, wondering what *that* must have meant.

I knew, though.

Frankfurt.

Blips of memories threatened to take me back there again, to that place I'd left so many years ago but still carried with me, somewhere unseen—wretched faces, demon lovers, grotesque angels. That was how I saw it now, all these years later. Our time there could be described as Caligulan. Raw. Primal.

Part of me had wondered if Frankfurt were the reason Andres had said yes to my request.

A bigger part of me wondered, if that *were* the reason, was this a punishment for me or a reward?

I might have some clarity around the former. But I still wasn't sure about the latter.

He turned toward me, his massive, barrel chest and intense eyes waiting for me to say something, do something. Almost daring me.

I couldn't help but wonder if the isolation—or the months of ayahuasca use he'd just copped to—could be taking a toll on him.

He *seemed* solid, head on straight. But in my short time in television—not to mention my much longer time in the culinary worlds I'd walked through—you could never really be sure.

Especially with the talent.

I brushed that thought off for now. All of them. Frankfurt. Andres's time in the ayahuasca ceremonies, his mental agility. Stuck them in the darkness of my subconscious with all the other burned-out husks that littered the road that was my past.

We had bigger things to worry about right now than looking stupid on a television show nobody even knew existed.

Mainly, how to not die in the next few hours.

So I did what I did best. Pushed the questioning thoughts away.

"Anyway," Andres said, "can we get a move on? I'd like to be at the valley floor before daybreak."

Without waiting for anyone to answer, Andres slung his pack back over his shoulder.

He raised his nose up to the wind and gave us all a look. Then he nodded his head.

As we walked toward the copse of trees across the clearing, I tried to mentally prepare myself for whatever we were about to face. I fell in behind Andres, letting the rest of our crew pick their own spots.

The tingle of imminent danger danced around under my clothing. Despite the chill in the air, I was already sweating. I adjusted my pack on my back, pulled the straps tighter so it fit my back as tight as I could make it. Opened the front zipper of my jacket to get some ventilation. Put my hands in, making sure my gloves were still there if it got colder. Adjusted the sheath at my back to make sure it didn't dig any farther. Pushed the inside pockets of my pants down so there would be no chafing as we walked.

I was scared, fidgeting.

Terrified, really.

The moon emerged from behind the clouds in what could only be described as a triumphant manner.

I had to shield my eyes from its brightness. It was so unfiltered and raw. I'd never seen it like that before.

I could practically smell the moon dust.

As we reached the edge, it illuminated the bowl of the valley below us. The sight was breathtaking.

Hopefully Nate was getting a good shot of this.

I didn't have time to ask him.

A single wolf howl rang out from the below, echoing across everything the moonlight touched.

It was deep. Hoarser than any wolf I'd ever heard before. Like one that had swallowed a Black Sabbath bass rift.

Before long, an entire macabre chorus joined the first.

Werewolves, I presumed.

And we were walking right toward them.

SEVEN

Our descent into Werewolf Valley, as Andres called it, was anticlimactic. Or, I suppose, pre-climactic would be a better word for it.

The country itself lived up to Andres's description.

It was rugged and very dangerous, each step a careful equilibrium between balance, pushing through fatigue, and speed to get through it. Even more so than the way up to the clearing because there was an even greater risk of tripping and falling down toward broken bones.

Or worse.

At least on the way up, your center of gravity leaned you toward the mountain. The way back down did not carry the same luxury.

But we all made it in one piece.

Nestled into a grove of Angel's Trumpet trees—so-called due to their large, fragrant, white flowers that resemble an angel Christmas tree topper—we waited quietly while Andres assessed the surrounding landscape. According to him, we were not yet in werewolf territory, merely on its edges.

But he was certainly being cautious.

As he looked around, I did the same. The surrounding jungle was breathtaking in its beauty and intimidating in its vastness. Even down here on the valley floor, the moon shone bright through the thick tops of trees, casting everything around us in an eerie white glow.

The Angel's Trumpets overpowered with their fragrance. Especially given how heavy I was breathing now that we'd descended thousands of feet in a matter of hours. Huddled beneath the glowing, bulbous flowers, it almost felt like we had string lights hanging over us.

Which didn't seem like a good way to *avoid* werewolves.

I tried not to think about that. Instead, I focused on breathing, trying to inhale slowly to both replenish my earlier lack of oxygen and to try and calm my nerves. My exhales turned to vapor ahead of me. It was warmer down here than up at the higher altitudes. Stickier air. But still not warm, though the exertion from the climb down was enough to hold off the chill for now, as the wind had since died down, unable to blast us in our hidey-hole on the valley floor.

Flittering leaves above us belied small birds, maybe. Branches moved, snapped, knocking into one another. Small, punctuated bursts of movement. The only indication we hadn't walked onto a movie set. Maybe animals moving, maybe just the trees settling.

But through it all, there was again that eerie quiet I'd noticed up on the clearing. We were in the middle of a thick jungle. Wilds untouched by major human intervention or pollution. It should have been teaming with life, with bugs, with the sounds of the night. Instead, it was almost perfectly quiet.

The animals must know something was going down.

And they had either gotten out of Dodge or hunkered down to avoid it.

"OK," Andres finally said, turning to us so as to keep his voice low, "we can keep moving."

Everyone nodded.

"We'll go that way." He pointed toward a ridge that rode up the right side of the valley. "Better vantage points."

We started walking, picking our feet over tangles of branches and bushes.

The ground was firm but moist. Andres had said it was good for us. We'd make less noise if we weren't stepping on dry branches and leaves while sneaking up on our quarry.

Which made sense to me. But I worried that it also meant we wouldn't hear something sneaking up on us, either.

It took us nearly an hour to reach the ridgeline, which seemed both impossible and completely normal. There were no paths to follow, no marked trails. Andres, perhaps, could see things that I couldn't. But even still, we weren't exactly walking over sidewalks.

On the ridgeline, the moon still hung like a flashlight above us in the sky, but I could see that its brightness was beginning to wane.

We had only an hour until sunrise.

Andres took out his binoculars and scoped out the valley floor below us, slowly scanning back along the way we'd come and past the direction we would be continuing on.

I wasn't sure what he was looking for. And I wasn't sure if it was a good or bad thing that he didn't seem to be finding it.

"Now we'll go there," Andres said, raising his finger up along the top of the ridgeline toward a flat, rocky area at the base of a sheer cliff face that rose up hundreds of feet before blending into the mountains that rose up into the sky off to our right.

"What are we looking for?" I asked, keeping my voice as low as his. Normally I would go with the flow but everything leading up to this point had sufficiently scared the hell out me. And I craved the false comfort of a plan.

As if that would mean a damn thing out here.

"A camping spot," he said. "Rest early in the morning, recuperate. The place I have in mind is close enough to their territory that we won't have much farther to go tomorrow night, before the moon rises. But not so close that we chance running into any of the bastards."

That was something like a relief, I guess.

After another look around, we all followed behind Andres. I took another look at my comrades on this journey.

Nate's expression was unreadable. He was panning the camera across the lower part of the valley we'd just emerged from, his face hidden by the lens and the camera equipment.

I took it as a good sign that he was doing his job instead of freaking out.

Maybe I should take a page from his book.

Lucy, still stoic and beautiful, didn't look the least bit concerned, either.

Part of her demeanor reminded me of a documentary I'd seen once about a special forces sniper who, during a training exercise in which he was submerged in sixty-degree water, eventually had to be pulled from the water by the medical staff. He'd passed into unconsciousness and his head fell below the surface, despite the fact he never started breathing hard or made any outward indication that he was under undue stress.

His heart rate barely rose above his normal resting rate.

When asked about it, a military doctor said it was common for that to happen to special forces soldiers because they were used to dealing with such a high level of stress that sometimes, they didn't even realize how something like that—something that would bring a normal person to immediate tears—was affecting them.

I didn't know if Lucy had dealt with particularly high levels of stress in her life, but she seemed to be dealing with this one just fine. A quick glance at Nate told me that same about him.

Again I wondered if they really weren't scared or if they were not truly understanding the risks.

Was I even understanding them?

One look at John told me that he was more aligned with me.

He looked ... haunted at the prospect of what we still had to face. Cheeks slicked with sweat, his hat having been pushed back on his forehead to let some cool air in, he looked terrified. And more than a little sick.

Or maybe it was the moonlight.

"Let's go," Andres said and set off in the direction of the rocks.

I turned to follow, unsure what else to do or say.

Getting to the rocks was an easier trip than any so far. Andres took a route that brought us down on either side from the very top of the ridgeline, a precaution he said was to avoid us being silhouetted against the sky.

"Anything below us looking up would spot us easily."

I didn't have the energy to ask him what could be looking for us that would be of concern if we weren't yet in werewolf territory.

I figured I didn't actually want the answer.

The vegetation, too, wasn't as thick up here. So the walk was over thinner patches of grass or wet dirt in places where heavy rains must have dragged away part of the ridge from the top down.

The faint orange and purple of a new day peeked through a slit between the mountains directly ahead of us. It was a breathtaking sight.

And a great relief.

"First night in Werewolf Valley," Andres said, falling in to walk beside me.

I nodded, unsure of what to say.

"Beautiful, isn't it?"

"If not a bit intimidating."

"Nature is nothing if not that."

As we approached the rocky area, I noticed it was not a flat spot at the base of a sheer vertical cliff like I had previously thought.

Instead, it was more like a ceremonial ground.

Each stone laid with care.

Constructed of thousands of black-grey stones, the ceremonial ground stretched nearly fifty yards out from us in a massive, perfect circle.

We stood at the edge of the stones, still on the grass.

I stepped onto the stones. The first level of them, at least.

Two additional levels—raised like stadium seating—ringed

around the edges, each overlapping with a different part of the perfect circle of the flat, first level. Both the second and third level, however, partially overlapped with one another. Creating what, from above, I assumed was some kind of crescent shape.

"What ... is this place?" I asked, feeling goosebumps forming up my arms. It was overwhelming, the precision with which the stones were laid, each one carved to perfectly fit next to the others. In the same way that seeing the pyramids shocked a modern audience, so too did this place, hidden in the folds of the Andes Mountain range.

Nate fanned out around us, getting a shot of the area. Lucy and John stayed out of the frame and behind us.

When Nate turned back to me, Andres said. "Welcome to the Temple of the Moon."

In the middle of the circle was a ritual stone of some kind. A perfectly polished, almost shiny-black semi-circle, topped with another stone cut into oddly shaped angles and planes. Atop both of those was a pillar that rose ten feet into the sky.

Whatever this was, it looked ancient as hell.

Visions of *Indiana Jones* danced through my head.

"Worth the trip, eh?" Andres said, his smile growing as the sunlight began pouring through the slit in the mountains and into the valley like a river spilling over a broken dam.

"Yes ... I ... it ... is." I was stunned. Speechless from the sheer magnitude of this place. The ceremonial ground was situated in a place where the mountain rose almost completely vertical from the valley floor, creating a backstop behind and above us.

It felt like being inside a massive sports arena, backed on one side by a cliff face. With your back to the cliff, though, the entire valley stretched out before us.

I walked across the stones and turned around, almost getting vertigo from the vertical ascent.

Before I could say—or stammer—anything else, Andres's smile dropped away.

He was looking over my shoulder, toward the direction of the ritual stone. Toward the jungle where he'd indicated the werewolves lay in wait.

Behind him, I noticed Lucy and John looking that way as well.

I turned around.

Despite all we'd been through that day, all of it fell away as soon as I saw her.

Walking toward us was the Amazon, her long, dark hair flowing gently as she moved. Her body was a shimmering wave of curves and wild, animal sensuality.

I ached at the sight of her, made even worse by the fatigue and hunger that the adrenaline of finding the Temple of the Moon temporarily pushed away from my conscious mind.

As the sun rose higher over the mountains, bathing the valley floor in a rising mist, Quille, as Andres had called her, walked right up to us and spoke with a voice that I instinctively wanted to hear forever.

"You made it in one piece, I see," she said, sauntering through and around our group with the quiet confidence of a predator.

"What are you doing here Quille?" Andres asked.

"I could ask you the same thing."

She stopped walking. She wore tight fitting clothing—dark colored khaki pants and a dark long sleeve cotton shirt revealing the curves of her body that struck my throat like a terrible thirst. Dressed in considerably less than the rest of us, only a pair of worn hiking boots and a small technical pack completed the look.

For a long moment, no one said anything.

Then Quille spoke.

Her cheekbones and nose created a visual vortex, commanding my attention toward her smoky dark eyes. They seemed to burn into me.

Made me suddenly self-conscious in a way I hadn't felt since a teenager.

"Now that you're all here, is anybody hungry? Because I'm starving."

EIGHT

We ate in silence, placing the thin foam mats we'd rolled up in our packs beneath us to keep our bodies warmer than if we sat directly on the cool earth or the ceremonial stones.

Breakfast wasn't glamorous. Cold bacon and handfuls of spiced nuts. Nothing befitting a world-class chef, but it was what Andres had brought with us on the journey.

There wasn't much about this situation that made sense to me anymore. Including what the hell John and I were thinking bringing our group into this mess.

I looked over at my old friend. He didn't look back at me, or even seem to notice. He simply chewed his food absently. It felt to me that he was in some other place ever since we left the clearing atop the mountain. His eyes were far off, wandering somewhere I couldn't see. Like a World War I soldier returning home.

Nobody spoke as we ate.

In fact, as I looked around, everyone on the New York crew looked tired. Sunken faces, drooping eyelids. Mouths about the only thing moving.

Andres was quiet. Not tired necessarily. But not his usual self.

I couldn't be sure what he was thinking.

Nor could I be sure about the odd exchange between him and Quille when she first arrived. He seemed surprised to see her.

Not happy, which I found odd.

Surprised.

But everyone here at our makeshift camp seemed to defer to Quille. Even those of us who had no reason to.

She was the only one of us not sitting, her lithe legs slowly walking around the ceremonial ground as she watched us. I couldn't remember if she'd eaten, I had been so caught up in my own food. Now that I looked at her though, food fell away from my mind.

But a different kind of hunger kicked in.

"What is this place?" I finally asked, unable to take my eyes off her. I figured Andres might know the answer to my question. Might even know it better than Quille.

But I didn't care. I was craving her voice again.

Craving her attention.

"This is *Killahuatana*," she said, the accented words dripping with carnal power. "Believed by many to be a pre-Incan ceremonial ground."

"Pre-Incan?" Lucy said. She'd looked up, finished with her meal, and was already working the sound equipment to capture Quille's audio, since the mysterious woman was the only one not already wearing a microphone.

Quille nodded. "The native peoples of this region—Incan and pre-Incan alike—as a whole worshipped the sun. From thousands of years before Christ, all the way up to the mass casualties of the mid-16th century, people in this region believed the sun god provided all things, from rain to crops to the divine offspring that founded Incan culture."

"So this was all built to worship the sun?" I asked.

Quille shook her head and gave me a tight smile that made me glad I was sitting down.

"Inti*huatana*, is the ritual stone and ceremonial ground of the sun god. Found at Machu Picchu. This is Killa*huatana*, found in an obscure, practically undiscovered region of the mountains. At least in this modern day."

"So ... different names. What does that mean?"

"It means the people who built this hallowed ground did not worship the sun. They worshipped the moon."

A chill ran through me as I took another look around the site.

"*Intihuatana*, the ritual stone at Machu Picchu, is sometimes referred to as the hitching post of the sun. The Inca thought the stone held and guided the sun in its travels across the sky."

"And the people who built this place?" I pointed to the ritual stone. "They believe that stone had the same function for the moon?"

She shook her head no.

"The people who broke from the Incas, they weren't peaceful settlers happy to break free from their brothers and sisters and co-worship a different deity in peace. They were a violent sect who believed the Moon was the giver of all things. But that it especially was the goddess of darkness."

I nodded.

Quille continued. "The particular kind of darkness that sits inside mankind. Darkness of the soul."

This scared me, for some reason. Not one for superstition, I felt a strange energy emanating from this place now.

"Of course, this sect did not stop with worship of the Moon," Andres said.

I turned to him. He lifted his massive form off the ground with incredible grace and dexterity. We were approximately the same age, but he moved much differently than me. Better, for sure. But with a smooth power that I envied.

Perhaps because he climbed mountains and I rode in elevators.

He went on, stretching himself slowly as he circled around us. "It is believed this sect, as they became hunted and persecuted, first by the Incan society they broke from and later by the Spanish conquistadors, turned toward darker pathways in order to protect themselves.

"Unfortunately, much like the Inca, no one has ever found any record of a system of writing. But the belief is that these people—these moon worshippers—somehow found a kind of dark magic that turned them, either by accident or by design, into werewolves."

I could hardly believe what I was hearing. Nate had by now started manning the camera again, so I could not read his face. Lucy was making sure the sound quality was coming in, so she was distracted.

John, however, was now looking up at Andres. A terrified look had possessed his pale face. I suddenly became deeply, intensely worried about him.

"So you're saying they became this way, maybe on purpose?" My mind was awash with questions and laced with fatigue.

"It's very likely. It would have been an advantage to them to become so vicious. In my travels, I've found rudimentary cave paintings in this valley that indicate mass slaughters that occurred. Primitive depictions of dead bodies, accompanied only by a black mass scratched onto the wall. An amorphous force capable of so much death that no survivor could ever truly say what it was."

I shuddered. "How many of them are left?"

Quille shrugged. "It's too difficult to tell. By night, we are lucky to kill one, maybe two. By day, the men of this ancient sect are not stupid. They can blend in, live off the land. This valley stretches for kilometers in every direction, almost impossible to search in full because of the land masses and conditions."

That didn't sound promising.

John raised his hand to say something but stopped. It was the first sentient movement I'd seen from him in hours.

"Are you alright, John?" I asked.

He shook his head. "We should leave. Now, while it's still light."

I looked at Andres. Then Lucy and Nate. None of them moved a muscle.

Then I turned to Quille.

I didn't want to leave her, as strange as that seemed. Where I'd been tired before, I now felt strong and alert. Perhaps it was my body returning back to normal, though I felt better than normal.

When we arrived, I had told Andres that we wanted to capture the kind of lifestyle he was living here. That it was different and important. All this time, we hadn't taken a single phone call or checked the internet.

Here we were in nature. Of nature.

And against it.

Quille said, "The quarry you all are after are ancient beasts of the most dangerous kind. It would be no shame if you left now, with what's coming."

"The Wolf Moon?"

She nodded.

It was our out.

But ...

"Hold on," I said, hoping that uttering those words would actually stop the flow of information and help me arrange my thoughts. But they were muddled.

Mixed into all of this, of course, was the fact that Quille was now less than ten feet away from me. I found myself intoxicated by her beauty, my desire for her flesh like jolts of electric currents dancing beneath my skin, desperate to get out.

This was no ordinary woman, which was already obvious to me. But the intensity of my lust for her felt like a curse. Like something inside me would explode if I didn't just *have* her. I'd never felt this way before. As if something had come undone inside me when she first appeared.

I turned away, which felt like pulling two strong magnets apart.

To Andres, I said, "You just said something about the commonly held belief about these ancient people. The, uh, moon-worshippers. Who believes that? I thought this was a site that was practically unknown to the world."

"It is."

Quille put her hand on my shoulder. I tensed as her lips brushed the edge of my ear.

"My people," she said. "We are the ones who know of this place. Of its history. Its bloodshed, soaking these lands."

Her voice buckled my knees. I wanted to lean into her. Grab her and run off into the forest.

"I don't understand."

She moved around to the front of me, closing off the rest of the world from the vortex of her beauty.

"We hunt these beasts, the ancient ones that still remain stalking this valley."

"We?"

For the first time since I saw her, Quille's face changed from strong and confident to sad.

"Force of habit," she said. "I hunt these beasts. My people no longer exist. Our sworn enemy—*these werewolf beasts*," she said these words with great hatred on her tongue, "—their sect is nowhere near as powerful these days because of the sacrifices and battles my people have had with them over the years. But I fear that now, without any help, their numbers will once again grow. And their powers will grow with them."

"Quille is the last of her kind," Andres said. "Or she was, until I showed up. After my quest, I ended up here. Was drawn to this place from the visions I saw in that last ayahuasca ceremony. A raven-haired woman. Alone in the Andes. Being hunted by werewolves, and worse. Her only refuge that of a strange ceremonial ground that held onto the darkness inside man's souls."

So that was the reason he'd stayed.

This was all so much to take in.

And I hardly had a moment to do so.

War cries rang out all around us, echoing off the cliff face at our backs and around the wide bowl of the valley.

I turned around, unsure where or what I was looking for.

It took me a while before I saw them. But once I did, I could see they were everywhere. They bled out of the jungles, walking slowly toward us as we froze in place on the ceremonial grounds.

More war cries. The tree line around us came alive with them.

They wrenched my stomach.

I looked over at Nate and Lucy, both of whom had stopped what they were doing for the first time since we'd started.

Finally scared.

And not a moment too soon.

NINE

John had been right.

We should have left.

By nightfall, it was clear that our show would never quite make it off the ground. Hard to get picked up by a major network when your entire cast and crew is dead.

Tied up by thick, rough rope made from braided jungle leaves, we six of us sat in a circle around the *Killahuatana* ritual stone in the center of the stone platform. Out in the open with no real chance of escape.

The group of us—Andres and Quille included—had been caught off guard.

Our captors—all men as far as I could tell—had emerged from the tree line like ghosts. Had they not been screaming like banshees, it's quite possible I wouldn't have seen them until they decided to ... well, do whatever it was they came here to do.

I didn't know what that was exactly.

But I was fairly certain they didn't intend to engage us in a tickle fight.

For a long time, we sat in silence as the men watched.

They were dark-skinned, similar to Quille. The color of caramel. Only their skin was the same texture as a catcher's mitt. Most of them were short but lean with sinewy muscles that looked more like a marathon runner's than a sprinter's.

None of them had the stereotypical war paint that one might expect to see in a Hollywood depiction of South American natives. They wore mostly a mishmash of clothes, from shorts to sweatpants to cotton and twill. One of them even wore a long-sleeve New York Mets Subway Series shirt from the ill-fated World Series they played against the Yankees. Under normal circumstances it might have been comforting to see. A slice of home all the way down here.

In these circumstances, it was terrifying, especially since it looked like the shirt had been worn every day since the year 2000 when it had obviously been made. As it was, it was practically faded to match the background colors of the wilderness.

At least it was useful for somebody.

All of these men seemed anxious. But after they tied us up, none of them seemed to walk on the ceremonial stones. They simply paced around us, eyes alternately on our group and on the skies.

Waiting for something.

Occasionally, one of them would start grunting or yelling and get the rest of them all riled up. I had visions of them storming us on the *Killahuatana* and ripping us to pieces. Leaving me for last while they roasted the others over a fire.

As if I wasn't scared enough, my mind had apparently decided to find new depths to plunder within my psyche.

In the last hour, as the sun began to splinter in the sky and touch the tips of the mountains, these men had gone from anxious to something else entirely.

One of them, the apparently leader of the group, started barking out commands to the men, who seemed to assent as they responded in kind with clipped, aggressive sounds more suited to a dog than a man.

The leader—who I started calling Easy Rider in my head, since he wore a bandana around his forehead and had the crazed look of Dennis Hopper in just about anything I'd ever seen him in—was a bigger man than the rest of the group, with a thick, corded neck that looked like he'd just walked out of a personal injury casting call.

He had beady black eyes and big teeth that he kept running his tongue against as he watched us, squirming around in our seats because our legs, backs, and asses had already fallen asleep.

"Andres," I said, keeping my voice low enough so none of our captors would hear us, though I was almost certain they didn't speak any English.

He turned his head toward me only slightly, his eyeballs moving to the periphery to let me know he was listening. We had only been able to make the slightest of communication or speech to one another because we were being watched so closely.

I just hoped none of these bastards were watching us right this second.

"Who are they?"

He looked at me cockeyed. Cut his eyes back toward the circle of men around us, most of whom, I now noticed, were looking in the other direction or talking quietly amongst themselves.

"These are the werewolves, Benjamin. In human form, called the Order of the Moon. In English, at least. In their language, its pronounced, *Killah*."

I shuddered.

"And, my dear Benjamin, that's exactly what they intend to do to us."

"Why won't they come onto the stones?"

He shrugged. "I've never had the pleasure of talking to them, so I don't know for sure. But Quille says it's superstition. They're worried that the ceremonial grounds are unclean during the daylight hours. It is only at night, when the moon is in position in the sky above us, that its light basks this place in the safety of *Killah*."

I watched as the men around us continued to agitate. There was no question that this stone held human darkness in it, just by way of the fact that we were sitting on it.

And our fate was looking awfully dark at the moment.

"Why the hell did you bring us here?" I asked, barely able to keep my voice low. Andres hadn't said a single word about any of this until it was far too late.

I felt pure, blind outrage. Plain and simple.

Of course, it ignored an equally simple fact. That part of me had wanted to come into this valley. Wanted it badly enough to fly across the world on a wild goose chase. Only this time we found the goose.

One of our captors howled into the air, breaking the quiet that had fallen over the ceremonial ground.

A chorus of man-howls followed, each one amplifying the violent electricity in the air and deep through the valley. The echoes brought the sound back upon us in stereo, the howls growing darker, deeper. Like some unseen force was twisting the EQ knobs.

"What are they doing?" I asked.

"They are preparing," Andres said. "It is almost dark. And soon they will transform beneath the Wolf Moon. The longest night of the year."

"Then what?"

"Then they'll do what they do best. Hunt."

Christ.

I glanced around the ritual stone, trying to make eye contact with any of the crew. Everyone's head was down. Keeping their own counsel. Taking their own final inventory.

I guess this was how it would end.

In the sky, I could see the faint outline of the moon. The breath-taking kaleidoscope of colors was fading through the mountaintops.

Our time was running out.

The howling continued, our captors lathering themselves into a frenzy of activity as they danced and grew increasingly rabid.

I didn't know what was happening. But I could tell it wasn't good for us.

Beneath the chorus of howls, I heard crying.

Quiet whimpers at first. And then, as the howls grew to a sickening fever pitch, the whimpers became sobs.

I craned my neck to see John start to lose it.

Always the dramatic one.

"John," I said, dispensing any of the whispering subterfuge we'd had to use earlier. None of our captors were paying attention anymore, anyway. "Keep it together, man. We aren't through with this yet."

"Aw hell," John said through thick sobs. "We're deader than the dead. Only thing left for us is to be ripped to pieces by these otherworldly *monsters*."

He was probably right. But for the purposes of the rest of our (potentially) short lives, I wasn't interested in going out like that.

"Calm down, John," Quille said. She *did* keep her voice down. Conspiratorial. "We have an opportunity coming up here. When the sun goes down."

"When the sun goes down, they're going to turn into flesh-hungry beasts," John said. "They're going to rip us into pieces. Even those stupid berries won't help us!"

"Think, John," she said.

"Think about my imminent death? Thank you, I had been contemplating the deep mysteries of the earth these past few hours. What a lovely and novel idea."

"Think about what will happen when the moon rises high in the sky."

"I don't bloody know! You and that crazy fool Andres are the only ones who hang about this insane place."

Quille waited a beat. "They will change into the beasts. And when they do, that will be our chance."

"Our chance?" I said. "Chance for what?"

"For escape," Quille said. "Our one and only. And if you're smart, you'll run like hell for that opening in the trees. The one in front of us."

I didn't see the opening because I was facing the opposite direction.

"*That's* your plan?" John said, almost yelling now. "You two come out here and get captured by these monsters, for what? For shits and giggles? To practice your sprinting?"

"John, quiet down. And we didn't get captured by them," Quille said, "We allowed ourselves to be captured."

"Allowed?" I said, turning around as much as I could so I could see Quille and John. "What do you mean *allowed?*"

Andres looked over at me.

"Sorry, Benjamin." He winced. "But you did owe me one from Frankfurt."

Those words smacked me like a pair of leather gloves. Frankfurt again? What was it with Andres? He kept bringing up the two-decade old memory that, for whatever reason, just wouldn't stay buried.

"If you wanted me dead, you could have just killed me back at camp. Now you'll have all our blood on your hands." The hair all over my body stood up as the howling continued and cool darkness fell over everything.

The sun had just fallen behind the horizon.

The howling grew to a new fever pitch.

"Get ready," Quille said.

The howling gave way to yelping as the dark forms of our captors fell to the ground all around the ceremonial grounds.

"Now!"

The surrounding rope tightened like a piano string around us. It dug into my chest, only prevented from cutting because of my thick clothing. Then the rope became slack and fell away.

"C'mon," Andres said, using a beefy hand to smack at my back and get my attention.

I looked around. Lucy and Nate were both on their feet.

Nate bolted for the camera, which our captors hadn't bothered to move far away from us. Probably thinking we were going to be puppy chow, anyway.

"Leave it!" I said.

Quille ran past me, following Andres toward a clearing in the tree line about fifty yards from where I stood.

But John didn't move an inch.

All around us, screaming, howling monsters squirmed in shadowed forms along the ground.

"John!"

He still didn't move. He was no longer sobbing or screaming, either.

He'd gone catatonic.

"Leave him," Andres called back from the trees.

I couldn't do that. I'd done that once already in my life, left behind someone who couldn't save themselves.

Back in Frankfurt.

And it haunted me still.

I ran around the ritual stone to John and grabbed him, trying to hoist him up to his feet.

He wouldn't budge.

"John!" I yelled into his face. Still no reaction.

I saw one of the shadowy forms go from a squirming ball on the ground to a knee, and then almost raising itself up to two feet.

I looked away, back to John. Not wanting to see anything more of what was happening here.

But John had the thousand-yard stare of a man whose fate was already sealed.

I pulled back my hand and slapped him across the face. That got his attention.

He looked at me with a mixture of confusion and pain. "What have we done?" he asked.

I ignored his question. There might be a time to talk about this.

But this wasn't it.

I pulled John up.
We both ran after the others.
Into the moonlit darkness.

TEN

Only we didn't run.

Not really.

Instead, once we reached the trees, Andres and Quille darted right and left, respectively.

My eyes followed Quille. Even in a moment of sheer terror, I could hardly take them off of her as she moved like an athlete through the trees.

She reached behind the trunk of a massive fig tree and pulled out a rifle. Eyes blazing white from the moon. Looking both terrifying and sexy at the same time.

"What are you looking at?" she said and handed me the rifle. She bent down and picked up another one.

When I turned around, Lucy and Nate were both holding rifles, too. Looking more comfortable than I would have expected.

Andres stepped from behind them, two rifles in either hand.

He handed one to John.

John didn't move, just looked at Andres. At the gun.

"I think you're going to want this, mate," was all Andres said, prodding him with an elbow to catch his attention.

The jungle came alive with the deafening chorus of werewolf howls and crazed barking from back near the ceremonial grounds. They'd apparently completed their transformation.

"Take it," Andres said to John.

Finally he did, the howls having brought him back to life a bit.

"Follow me," Quille said, running around three thick roots sticking out of the ground like the Loch Ness monster.

We followed, all of us in a line. I suppose it should have been obvious to me earlier, when we were tied up and held captive by the werewolf-men, that we were now prey in this jungle.

I had never thought of it, really. Call it a city-slicker's mindset. The realization that we weren't the only thing atop the food chain here. We might not even be on top at all. This new mindset was more terrifying than I cared to think about.

As we came through a clump of bushes that forced us to step high over them and into a small break in the thick foliage, a shadow raced by. It disappeared almost as quickly from the opening.

Quille took a shot at it, the rifle report breaking through the werewolf howls.

Leaves fluttered into the air and made a slow descent toward the ground.

The shadow kept going, almost too fast to comprehend. Quille had missed. Which was terrifying. Because she moved almost as fast as the shadow.

How the hell was I ever going to hit anything?

Behind us, Andres fired a shot at some unseen thing off to our left. Soon enough, Lucy and Nate had sprung into action, too. Their tall, lean bodies taking on the task like soldiers, using their hand-eye coordination to the fullest extent.

I was frozen in place though. My mind still trying to catch up to what was going on.

Trying to convince the rest of my body to do something.

Through an opening in the trees, I saw one of the horrific werewolf shadows.

It stood up, its eyes blazing with violence.

Against my better judgement, I actually marveled at it. Ogling like Andres had at Lucy. Or I had at Quille.

Except rather than having sex on the brain, I had only a chilling, paralyzing fear.

On two feet, the werewolf was eight feet tall. Taller than a lot of the trees around us. It had a barrel chest and arms that wouldn't have looked out of place on a pro linebacker.

Its face was matted with black, slick fur. Snout at least as long as my forearm, leading up to a prominent, furrowed brow line. Its eyes were those of a beast but with a certain cunning that could only be of man.

The werewolf opened its teeth to howl. All I could see were razor sharp teeth the size of railroad spikes.

It let out a guttural, fierce sound either deep inside its chest or the bowels of hell (maybe both). The sound grabbed me by the throat and squeezed, a little love-tap that would certainly signify the beginning of the end for me.

I suddenly felt a warmth dripping down my leg and soaking my socks.

The werewolf had been turned away from me, focused more on howling at the moon than on anything else around it.

But that only lasted for a moment.

It turned. Sniffed at the air. Looked at me, its massive body silhouetted against the grey night sky.

It took a step closer. Then another. As if it were deciding on a blitzkrieg attack to rip my head off or to pull me apart bit-by-bit like a cat playing with a fallen bird.

It was close now. Close enough that I could smell it. Its musk heavy and sour, the scent disbursed into the air from the moisture steaming off it. Wet, oily fur at least five inches thick and covering every part of its body.

It opened its mouth and I once again saw those railroad spikes. Two rows of them like a prehistoric sea creature. They looked sharp enough to cut glass.

I had no doubt they'd cut me just fine.

The werewolf got ready to strike out at me.

Arms extended out wide like a big, deadly hug. Snarling mouth ready to bite.

Saliva dripped from its powerful jaw. Moist, stinking breath blowing on my statue-still body.

In my paralysis, I hadn't even moved the rifle from where I'd slung it over my shoulder. I assumed it was loaded, but I didn't know for sure. I got the strong sense that any sudden movement from me would end very badly.

But hell, this wasn't going to end well either way.

I went for the rifle, trying to swing it off my shoulder and out, all in one motion. Like some gunslinger in a western.

Only I was a failed chef / failed television host / failed restauranteur from the city.

The rifle caught on my jacket, freezing in place. For a terrified moment, I thought maybe I would shoot my own damn self.

Instead the werewolf lunged forward, eyes and mouth wide. Arms ready to pull me in for a hug and not let go until I was mush.

Chunks of flesh blew out of a hole in its chest.

I didn't understand what happened at first.

It let out a horrific bellowing sound as it fell to its knee. It's body spasmed. Head snapped back. Each limb undulating like an inflatable tire man.

I had to step back just to avoid a sharp paw the size of a dinner plate that came flailing through the air, crashing down into the earth like a meteor where I'd been standing.

I watched as the hellish blaze of craven life left its eyes.

Then it fell to the ground with a thud.

Dead. Or so I hoped.

I turned and saw Quille behind me, rifle ready in case another shot was necessary. She winked. Then reloaded her rifle with a silver bullet to replace the spent round, pulled from her pocket and scanned around the area.

She'd saved my life. And all I could do was shake in shock at the prospect of still being alive. My muscles seized, then released in something akin to the power going off.

Ten feet behind her, Lucy and Nate stood, backs to one another, firing shots at unseen shapes in the thick woods. They moved like dancers, their faces lit orange as the muzzles flashed. I had no idea if they'd shot weapons before but if they hadn't, they had picked it up quickly.

I thought.

I wasn't entirely sure how much time had passed since we'd escaped from the ceremonial site.

It had seemed like forever.

Andres was near them, doing the same thing. It seemed I was the one who'd wandered away from the safety in numbers. He had told us to stay together.

He dropped to one knee to reload the silver bullets from his coat pocket. He was a picture of steady—hands gracefully moving from one moment to the next with the practiced assuredness of a man who'd done this all before. Eyes never left the area around him, never once looking down at what his hands were doing. Autopilot.

He stayed kneeling. Then fired from that position down into a gulley, his own face lit up by the muzzle flash. Full of the prehistoric rage I now realized was part of the allure of this place.

All around me, I saw my team—and thank God they were on my side, for I was useless—putting down these massive, rabid beasts which hit the ground like felled trees.

Their disturbed howling grew quieter as the choked sound of dying werewolves took its place.

The commotion rolled up on me in a tidal wave of inner heat, my body suddenly sweating beneath my gear, my pant leg no longer the only thing that was soaked.

All these sensations knocked my mind off-kilter. Sent it retreating into itself. Sharply. The way a rabbit retreats into its burrow when a fox turns up.

In an instant, I saw everything that had happened to lead us up to this point.

And all of the things I hadn't.

I saw Quille emerge from Andres's hut. Not in a post-coital glow but in the same way the spider sneaks away once its trap has been set.

I saw Andres alone in his small hut as we approached. Not because he'd shunned society, or he found more value in the strenuous life. But because he was trapped here. Needed a desperate group of ambitious people to take this journey halfway around the world on a lark in order to escape.

I saw Danner Winston—that sonofabitch—sitting across from me in that greasy alley hole-in-the-wall dumpling joint, his eyes faded as he spoke of the forbidden rumors he'd heard of Andres's new path in life. But instead of faded eyes from too much drink, I now saw them for what they actually were.

The dampening of his conscious as he laid this bait for me to take.

Finally, I saw Frankfurt. The parts that I'd pushed down and deep into the darkness of my subconscious. I had been treading water for years leading up to that fateful night. Living on the edge. Every vice at my fingertips. No discipline to shun them.

The events of that night lurked around beneath me like a great white shark.

Just waiting for the time to strike.

I saw the girl. How horrible it was I couldn't even remember her name. I watched as she drowned in that lake, my own body too paralyzed to do anything. Too cold to move. Too foggy to make any rational change to my own actions. Or lack thereof.

Andres had fallen beside me, his arm slamming into the ground as it connected solid with the ice that seemed to cover everything in the weeks we were there.

Watched myself cringe at the sound of his fall. Somehow that stuck out to me, rather than the girl who'd fallen through the ice and was screaming for one of us to help her. His fall ... as if his bone had been frozen solid and then shattered against the icy path along the lake's edge.

I saw the girl's grey eyes atop the glassy darkness of the black water. Despite the cold, the ice had been thin where we'd had her walk. Dared her to walk. Some stupid prank that had been lost in the haze of my drinking and drugging.

The ice had splintered. A larger piece broke off than I ever could have expected.

It was only by sheer luck that Andres or I hadn't been pulled into the water as well.

I saw her, watching then and now with detached horror as she slipped beneath the surface, just as the moon peaked out from behind the clouds and turned the water into a moving slick of silver that wiped her away from the land of the living.

I saw Andres years later, when the police came to question him. The horror on his face as they broached that topic that had for so long been pushed down inside him the same way it had been inside me.

I saw his rage as he fled to the South American beach bars, hustling to make ends meet by flipping arepas before they burned on the oily flat top in need of a permanent clean.

I saw all of those things slip away from him as he descended into the jungle to find some deeper meaning to the world. Meaning after such senseless tragedy.

Saw his soul while the ayahuasca drew new connections in his mind, painted them with a new set of brushes, the strokes creating colors and patterns that had yet to have been discovered.

Most of all, I saw myself during this whole journey. Saw the truth that I had refused to face. Saw my soft, posh life in the city. The desperate need to impress others, chase down the things that didn't really matter.

Saw the true driving force that refused to let me turn back. It wasn't a television pilot, that was just the excuse.

I'd been seeking something else here. Something much deeper. More primal.

I saw so many things in this final moment of panic in the Andes Mountains, as the few remaining werewolves screamed their blood-thirsty song and desperately thrashed around for flesh.

But there was one thing I didn't see. Perhaps the single thing that would haunt me worse than anything I'd yet done in my thrashed-out collection of experiences I called a life.

I didn't see John.

ELEVEN

I didn't have much time to contemplate everything I'd seen in my mind's eye.

A scream through the thick palm fronds off to my right brought my attention around.

Pulled me out of my head. And back to the present.

It was John's voice.

I ran toward it. Leaping over a short bush in my way and pushing blind through branches slapping at my face and neck.

When I finally saw John's face, it was in sheer agony. Its pale white sheen framed against the dense green and brown all around us.

A werewolf bigger than the one that had stood over me was hunched over John like the Andes mountains hunched over us.

It was biting his left leg.

Without thinking, I pulled the rifle from my shoulder and sighted it at the beast.

I pulled the trigger, the gun punching my shoulder and knocking me backward. Almost causing me to lose my balance.

The werewolf howled in pain as the shot tore through its massive, muscled back. Just as the other one had, it went down quickly afterwards, the silver bullets seeming to almost act as a poison against them.

Apparently the lycanberries hadn't worked, either, because he hadn't immediately let go of John's leg the way they were supposed to.

I could see that much from here. The bites were far worse than I thought—far worse than I could have ever imagined.

John's leg had been practically pulled from its socket.

I knelt next to him, his white face sweating and flecked with his own blood.

I looked at the wound. Though I wish I hadn't.

His leg was torn apart, bleeding from seemingly everywhere. It had been mangled all to hell. His muscles flayed by the razor-sharp teeth. I could see where even the bone had been chewed through.

"John," I said, "stay with me."

His eyes were wide, glowing silvery in the moonlight.

The lycanberries.

I rooted around John's pockets, searching for the pouch of them.

"You're going to be alright, John," I said, trying to keep the confidence in my voice. Based on what I'd seen from his leg, I had no idea if alright was even in the realm of possibility for him anymore.

I found the pouch and pulled it out of his pocket.

But John was already dead.

"Christ, John!"

He didn't say another word.

Just died in my arms like a dog.

"Benjamin!" Andres yelled.

I turned, my eyes hazy from the tears that had formed there from losing my producer. My friend. John was a good man. He didn't deserve to die like this.

Nobody did.

Rage coursed through me like a Class 5 Whitewater.

I stood up, and picked up my rifle, using my other hand to wipe away the tears.

Something changed in me then. It was as if the responsibility of killing this man lashed at me all at once.

I was furious.

It might have been my imagination, or the insane adrenaline rush, but I could see everything around me in stark, silver-hued clarity.

Ten feet away, two werewolves stood in a clearing. One had its nose up to the air. The other was scanning around like a soldier looking for his next target.

I shouldered the rifle and let loose two quick shots in succession. Hit the first werewolf center mass as he rose up to face me—his massive chest providing a large enough target that even I could hit it.

I only grazed the second werewolf, but it went down in a yelping hulk of mass.

I put the rifle's butt to my bruised shoulder and sighted on another, a werewolf stalking through the low grasses, moving away from me and toward Nate, who was busy firing shots into a leafy shrub.

My rifle clicked. But nothing came out.

I was out of ammunition.

All around me, the sounds of gunshots, howls, and screams punctured the still night air, sending a wave of panic through me.

How was I going to survive without a weapon? It seemed unlikely I would survive even with one.

"Benjamin!" Andres screamed again. "Behind you!"

I turned to see John, incredibly, on one knee. His good leg. The other hanging from a string behind him, splayed out on the ground. Hand outstretched on a bent palm branch. Almost to standing.

Thank God. Perhaps his injury hadn't been as bad as I thought. Maybe I'd hallucinated it in the melee.

"John!" I yelled, stunned and elated. "John, let me help you." I could hardly believe my eyes.

I went to him, prepared to get under his armpit and help him up.

He turned away from the tree, throwing himself toward me. I

tried to catch him. A sharp elbow struck my face. His other arm grabbing my back, trying to hold on.

But his strength—his inhuman strength—knocked me backward to the ground.

As I slammed into it, my own head snapping back, a terrifying realization hit me.

John was dead. The man I'd known was gone.

Whatever he was now was far worse.

He used the palm branch and stood up on two feet—his left leg buckling, then cracking beneath the weight of his body.

But he continued to stand tall, unaware of the pain.

He was larger now, standing taller and larger than even Andres. Back arched in a sickening, twisting motion reminiscent of a double helix.

The moon streamed through an opening in the trees behind him. Lighting him. Lighting this ... transformation. Creating a horrifying, giant silhouette as John raised his head and howled up at the moon, his voice morphing from man to beast mid-howl.

Had it not been so terrifying, I might have marveled at the sight.

Instead, as John turned to me—his eyes black chasms focused only on me, his face morphed halfway between the face of my friend and the snout of a werewolf—I realized one thing with startling clarity.

John now wanted to kill me.

I pushed myself back on my hands, away from the snarling monster, and tried to get up.

I tripped over the now inept rifle and almost knocked myself unconscious.

Before I turned back over. John was already upon me, raring his head back again and up toward the moon.

He growled, almost completely werewolf now.

His eyes were the last thing to go. A realization existed in them. A trepidation. A light. Like he was fighting some internal battle, trying to avoid the animal instincts now overpowering his will.

That light went dark as he turned to face me.

He looked hungry. And angry.

I fumbled in the dirt around me, looking for something, anything that might help me.

But I had nothing.

John moved closer, his now-beefy arms spreading wide in that hug of death I'd already seen more times than I'd needed to. Ready to crush me to death, swallow me whole, maim me. Just like he'd been maimed.

Whatever it took me get me good and dead.

I pushed myself farther back, a shooting pain in my lower back cutting through all the rest of what was going on.

I'd cut myself.

John closed the distance again and lowered his snout to my chest, taking one last sniff of his quarry before devouring me.

His breath smelled like brimstone.

Then he snapped his body back like a whip and dove his open, snarling mouth at my head.

TWELVE

I snapped my wrist, driving the silver-plated knife from my back into John's eye. Up to the hilt.

The silver worked instantly. Though I imagine my placement would have put him down even if the knife had been made of copper.

I was glad I didn't have to find out.

Because John the werewolf was one scary creature.

He made a low whimper for a second and then fell forward, his momentous weight landing on top of me. He stank like the rest of them, his oil-slicked fur coating me in his scent. Suffocating me with it.

I didn't move for several seconds, praying that John the werewolf was actually dead.

His dead weight certainly seemed to indicate that he was.

The adrenaline faded. That was when the pain came crashing back down on me.

The spot in my back where my own knife had stuck me ached something sharp and fierce. It was hot, deep. Near my spine. Made even worse with the added pressure from John's weight. But I was lucky.

I was alive.

More than I could say for my friend.

Gunshots punctuated the night air. It sounded like Andres, Quille, Nate, and Lucy were still taking care of the rest of the werewolves. I hoped being hidden beneath one would keep me safe for now.

The pain in my back leveled off. The worst of it having already knocked my nerves into submission. It still hurt like hell, but I couldn't stay here. I was vulnerable.

I made an attempt to squeeze my way out from under John's massive frame. As I did, I tried to keep alert. Eyes up, searching the area for movement. Letting the sounds of the forest wash over me, listening for anything that might be approaching.

The cadence of the gunshots died down, slowing to a few inconsistent shots. Then finally drawing to an end. What followed was a complete and total silence.

I slid out from beneath John and slowly—biting back the pain—got to my feet. A rush of blood to my head told me that was far too quick of a movement, and I leaned against the palm branch that John had used to stand up after his death.

The sight of his blood all over the ground should have made my stomach lurch. Especially coupled with the memory of what I'd seen.

His mangled, practically amputated leg.

And his white, terrified face.

That should have made me wretch.

Should have made me cry.

Brought me to my knees with guilt. It was my idea to come here. *I* was the one who pushed us—all of us—to bet on this trip for my own selfish reasons. Using the show as bait for the rest of them. I could have listened to John's warnings, waited until we had more time to research the area and the legends surrounding it. Or simply faced up to my own shortcomings and fears.

I'd been trying to prove something to myself with this journey.

And John had died because of it.

All of emotions should have gone through me.

But they didn't.

Next to the blood-spattered snow angel—the aftermath of John's first death—lay the beast that had killed him. Just like John the werewolf, it lay perfectly still, its body in a state of agonized repose.

I went to it, bit my lip in preparation for the pain from my self-inflicted wound, and heaved my weight against the beast.

It hardly moved. Must have weighed a thousand pounds.

I heaved again. Same result.

"Benjamin?" Andres's voice carried through the cool, quiet air. I had no idea what time it was now, though I sensed it had grown darker from when the moon touched the top of the sky. We were past the winter solstice now. The Wolf Moon would be on its descent, not to be seen again until this time next year.

I wondered what would become of this place now that all the werewolves were gone.

Maybe it would return to some kind of equilibrium. Small creatures would return first. Bugs. Then birds. Rodents. Then larger things—monkeys, javelina. Perhaps even pumas.

The air no longer smelled like werewolf, their musky, oily scent no longer being pumped into the air.

Now it only smelled of gunpowder and coppery blood.

"Benjamin!"

Lucy's voice.

Then Nate's.

I kept my mouth shut as I looked around the area. I found a fallen tree branch, thick as my upper arm and about the length of my leg. A perfect lever.

I slide it as best I could beneath the dead werewolf, forced a rock beneath it, and once again heaved my weight, trying to move the beast that killed John.

It still hardly moved.

But this time, hardly was just enough.

I knelt down and reached my hand beneath it.

Slid out John's rifle.

I returned noiselessly to John the werewolf's body. I was suddenly aware of every silence between the spaces around me. It was as if I was wired to the sounds of the jungle.

I pried my knife from John's eye socket, the slurp of his brain matter and flesh the only sound for miles, beside the quiet, cautious footsteps of Quille, Andres, Nate, and Lucy.

I wiped the brain matter and flesh against my pants.

I reached my other hand behind me for the sheath, careful to avoid the place where the knife had cut me.

I pulled the sheath off my belt. It would probably be useless now, the knife having ripped through it before cutting me.

I looked at it beneath the moonlight. It was slick with dark blood.

But the sheath itself was perfectly intact. I slide the knife in just to check. Fiddled it around. No rips or places where the knife had punched through.

I looked at it for a long, long time.

If the sheath was intact, and the knife was still inside it when I reached for it to stab John, then the knife itself wasn't what had cut me.

"Benjamin!" Andres again.

Louder now.

Closer. He was circling out from his position.

Closing the distance.

Somehow I sensed this. The same as I could sense the silence. I could smell the fresh dirt, spores and bacteria churned up from all the commotion around us.

I looked out toward the direction of the voices, their pitches and timbres plucking strange, previously unknown strings inside me.

I saw every leaf, every detail. Strips of bark worn out by passing animals. Stems of flowers expanding, trying to inhale the extra carbon dioxide in the air.

I turned back to Benjamin the werewolf. Knelt down next to my friend.

Picked up his heavy paw. The one that had knocked me backward when I tried to help him.

It was covered with blood.

With my newfound acute sense of smell, I could tell it was my own blood.

"Oh God," I said to myself. "Oh, God, what's happened?"

But I knew.

A few feet away were John's clothes, the ones he shed when he turned into this horrible, massive beast.

The lycanberries. They would still be there.

I pulled at the shredded clothing, finding the pouch of berries. I poured them out into my hand.

And stopped.

"Benjamin!" The voices were closer now. I could practically see each of them, could sense their every step touching down onto the wet ground.

I hesitated, wanting to yell out to them. Wanting to eat the lycanberries and give myself a chance to stay in this modern prison I was desperately trying to escape.

But a much larger part of me didn't want that. Instead, the new wild cells inside me were howling, telling me that I'd finally found the true reason I'd come on this journey in the first place.

I'd become savage.

And free.

The berries in my hand represented only the life I'd lived so far, a soft life of excess and debauchery.

I stared at them.

"Benjamin!"

"Do it, call out to them," I said to myself.

But I stayed quiet. Took a long, deep breath.

Let the lycanberries drop from my hand onto the ground.

Sniffed at the air.

Turned and disappeared into the thick, savage jungle.

THIRTEEN

Do I regret my decision to turn my back on society and reconnect with my true nature?

I sit on a rocky finger above Werewolf Valley as the sun sets over the Andes, stunned by the vastness of nature stretching out below me.

I've stalked this valley for the last three hundred and sixty-four days. Day and night. As man and beast. I am one with nature. Not simply in it, but *of* it.

I eat only what I kill, having long ago lost my taste for anything but fresh meat.

The cool air feels sublime on my skin.

I am naked except for a ripped pair of shorts I strung back together, having scavenged them off a man living in a nearby mountain village who wandered into the wrong place at the wrong time. He ripped through them when he turned into a werewolf, my own hunger for his flesh having been the culprit.

We stalked together for days before *they* caught up with us.

Not surprisingly, Lucy and Nate stayed with Andres and Quille. Much like me, once they got a taste of this life, they couldn't let it go.

Turns out they weren't ambitious to get into television.

They were ambitious to live a life true to themselves and nature.

I've wondered on more than one occasion what would have happened had I eaten the lycanberries I'd held in my hand during the last Wolf Moon. I suppose we all would have had to go home. The werewolf threat would have been over.

As it stood, I guess we were all content with the decision I made.

Two shapes emerge before me, lithe and muscled. New members to my tribe. Savage, lethal bodies.

Like my own.

The sun falls lower into the sky, almost disappearing behind the line of mountains across the valley from us.

Soon the Wolf Moon will once again be visible.

I remember seeing it—really seeing it—for the first time last year. So big I felt I could touch it.

It is our savior. Our everything.

For it brings with it the darkness. And freedom.

And when the moon is full and bright, that is when we truly become ourselves.

So, do I regret my decision?

A fiendish energy courses through my blood. I stand up, stretch my muscles.

Arch my back and let out a hellish howl up to the darkening sky and Mother Moon.

What do you think?

FAMILY TREE

A SUSPENSE NOVEL

WRITERS OF THE FUTURE AWARD FINALIST

NIZ THOMAS

FAMILY TREE

A NOVEL

by Niz Thomas

EXCLUSIVE SNEAK PEEK

ONE

Joe Parry woke up with a jolt, like he'd just been struck with a cattle prod. His eyes shot open but it took him a second to register where he was. His heart was pounding against his chest like it was trying to escape. Or explode. For a brief second he wasn't sure it had a preference, though his would have been for whichever did the job faster.

He saw a single salmon-pink splotch of paint on the bedroom wall, peeking out from under what was otherwise a complete cover-up job. His daughter, Samantha, must have missed the spot last month when she sponge-painted the entire wall charcoal grey, part of a number of recent changes that Joe wasn't completely comfortable with. He didn't need another look at the nude art posters she'd hung above the eave of her desk for a reminder of that fact.

Joe tried to catch his breath. He'd been dreaming of something dark and ambiguous, a heavy weight of a feeling, like impending doom. Or an anvil on his chest. Unfortunately, he knew the feeling well. He'd had plenty of nights like it in recent years, though this one felt somehow different for him. Worse, sure, but also like the end of something that he hadn't known had started yet.

Turning his neck — which he realized, with some discomfort,

hadn't managed to find a pillow in the night — and he felt his heart rate slow a bit, knowing he was at least in his own house. He took a long, deep breath to reacquaint himself with the land of the living and inhaled the orange and lavender scent from the candle he'd bought Samantha two months earlier, and given to her last week for her eighteenth birthday. He felt ashamed now that he'd bought it so far in advance and upon giving it to her, it couldn't have seemed any stranger of a gift.

Even unlit, the smell was so potent it crept through his nostrils and settled deep in his throat, constricting his windpipe just enough to make him cough. Like a feminine version of chloroform.

That scent, and the thought of every moment since he'd first smelled it at the mall, hurt him more than any cattle prod could have. He could see now that two months could move mountains in a teenager's world. Even the two weeks since Samantha had turned eighteen had felt to him more like wrangling cattle than being one. Things started happening much faster and he felt like they needed to be contained.

He could never quite get his hands around the situation though.

Joe put his feet on the floor and slowly pulled himself up. His neck cried out something fierce at the effort and he felt a few muscles down his back and ribcage light up with their own protests, too. He let himself sit there, on his daughter's empty bed, the realization of her not coming home another night made it feel like he just woke up from a car wreck.

Five nights. Five of the longest nights he'd ever had — and that was saying a lot. He wondered if Samantha had ever sat up at night as a kid, waiting in vain for him to come home. He put that thought aside as quickly as he could muster in the cold of the empty room and the darkness of a fall morning. Talk about the shoe being on the other foot.

Sitting there, he picked up the cordless phone next to Samantha's bed. He'd brought it in from his room, just in case she called. It was the only phone in the house and he'd thought about getting rid of it for the last few years but never cared enough to do so. He checked the caller ID but saw there had been no missed calls. He put the phone back on the side table.

He became aware of the tick, tick, tick of his wristwatch. The rest of the house was silent. A far cry from the city sounds he'd spent most of his life cocooned in. There wasn't a single car horn or emergency siren to be heard. The sticks — as he referred to them, but in reality, what most people would call the suburbs — were far too quiet for him. It gave all the thoughts inside him more amplification than he liked.

He always could have used more of a chance to think before he acted. But sitting in silence, thinking about the worst? Well, that just wouldn't do for him.

Even after two years living in the sticks — a northern New Jersey town called Mendham — he didn't feel adjusted to the quiet. The town wasn't far from where he grew up in Newark, but it might as well have been in another country. The biggest commonality was that people breathed oxygen in both places. Most of Newark was rundown now, but it hadn't been so bad when he grew up there. It was a city of immigrants back then — Italians, mostly. By contrast, the houses in Mendham consisted of a few historic sites built by militia men during the Revolutionary War surrounded by lawyers' and bankers' mansions built sometime after the last bull market. The legacy was still alive, Joe supposed, but the reality was that, despite the fact that just a few miles away George Washington and his army camped during the winter of 1779, the only thing that still remained from that era was the quiet.

And sitting alone in the house his then-wife convinced him would be the salve on half-a-lifetime of putting the badge first, the silence of this place felt personal. Like it was made specifically to torture him. He wondered if any of those militia men had felt that, too.

He got up and smoothed out the bed's comforter, wanting the room to feel exactly how Samantha left it whenever she decided to come back home. Then he went to the threshold of the doorway and turned once more back to the room, wondering if he was being too naïve. If the thought of her coming back to him and this house wasn't more than a pipe dream.

The room looked so different now. Grey and black color had replaced the pinks and pastels from only a few months ago. But that felt like another lifetime at this point. Samantha's closet, neater than any kid's he ever knew, was more of the same color palette. Black and grey jeans and long tees replaced the rainbow colors of dresses and blouses. And a growing collection of nude art posters.

He closed the door and went downstairs.

In the kitchen, he set up the coffee. Samantha had taught him how to use the thing when she bought it for him a year earlier. It was one of those machines with more levers than it seemed to need — like Rube Goldberg's idea of a coffee maker. At the time, Samantha had been going through a "coffee phase" and he was pretty sure the gift had been more for her than for him. Either way, he had to agree with her. It tasted better than the watered-down version his old drip machine produced.

Joe opened the cabinet above the machine and reached past the decaf and lighter roasts for a brand called Unleaded Java. It was that type of morning. After loading the beans into the dispenser, he switched the machine on and it went to work grinding them up. It couldn't finish the cup fast enough for him.

He reached for the stereo remote and hit play, not sure what would come on. It had sat silent for the past five days. Since his wife left them, Samantha had always worked the stereo for him. While her taste in music didn't really match his, he felt it was something that brought them together. Especially before she decided coffee wasn't for her anymore, due to the injustices involved with making the beans, or whatever the issue of the day was.

The song that started up was faint at first, almost mechanical in its introduction. There was no singing or words yet, just a low humming sound mixed with the timbre of a factory — grinding metal and power tools. Definitely not the type of music that Samantha would have played six months earlier, but he guessed those days were long gone. At the moment, he didn't care about the music. He just wanted the noise. The song had an eerie quality mixed with the grinding of the coffee machine. It hearkened back to the days when people like him would have been working the factory floor, not much more to worry about than what the wife was making for dinner that night. But then, he guessed those days were long gone now, too.

Joe stood there, eyes closed, letting the sounds wash over him. For a moment, he fell into a trance, thankful for the brief respite from his own mind.

Once the machine was done, Joe took a big sip of the coffee, the bitter smell and taste bringing back the closed throat feel from the candle in Samantha's room. He hardly noticed, though, desperate to wake up. The song kept playing, growing in intensity, leading him toward something dark and mysterious. He felt like he was moving toward the end of a hallway in a horror movie.

His phone buzzed on his hip, making him jump and almost spill, and pulling him up and out of the trance-like state the music created. He lifted the remote and turned it off.

"Parry."

"Joe, it's Shea," the voice said. Shea Walters. With the music and the fog from a shit night of sleep on his mind, he'd forgotten she said she'd get back to him today. She was a private investigator who used to work undercover with him. A good, reliable cop, though she'd had a bit of a fall from grace in recent months, from his understanding of things. He knew the feeling well enough — his move out to the sticks wasn't *exactly* a self-less move — and he also knew a cop like Shea wouldn't let it get to her. He'd asked her to pull in a favor with a contact she had.

"Hey Shea, you got something for me?"

"Yeah, I'm doing great, Joe. Happy to help a friend in need."

"Sorry. My mind's a little fucked right now. She hasn't come home in five days. I'm just worried."

"Yeah, well, when kids turn legal, sometimes they rebel. My parents would have killed for me to just slip out of the house for a week. They still, to this day, don't believe I was a cop. I didn't have the heart to show them the newspaper clippings after I got canned, just to prove it to them. Try not to take it personal, Joe. It's probably more about her own thing than anything you did."

Joe wished that were true. He took another sip of the coffee, finally feeling it working on his cobwebbed brain, and went over to the sliding glass doors off the kitchen. Growing up, Joe could never have pictured himself living in a place like this. It was too green, too wholesome. He'd worked narcotics and then homicide for a bit in his hometown. The only green he saw was the money they took off the dope dealers when they popped them. The setting out here was more like something out of a Stepford brochure. Not even the dealers wanted to score big and live like this. He doubted they even had the imagination. And these were the same sort of people who started sculpting fake toys made out of cocaine to avoid detection.

He took another swig of the coffee, having a sudden hankering for a shot of Jameson in it. He stared out at his manicured backyard, the showcase piece of which was a twenty-five-foot tall chestnut tree that sprawled at least as wide, canopying the flowers and hedges planted in mulch on the back end of the property. A single rope swing hung from the tree's thickest branch, an addition he'd made on Samantha's fifteenth birthday. He could practically hear her laughter from that afternoon echoing through the quiet of the house.

It was thought to be one of the last surviving chestnut trees in the whole northeast. It was basically the reason they chose the house in the first place.

"You there, Joe?" Shea asked.

"Yeah, sorry. Just trying to stay positive, that she took off with a friend or something."

"I'm sure that's what it is, bud. I wish I had something to help ease your mind. Unfortunately, my contact came up empty. The phone's been off since Tuesday night."

An icy fear rose up in the pit of his stomach. That was the last night he'd seen Samantha. The night of her birthday. He wasn't all that surprised that she hadn't turned it back on yet — other than being a teenager and have the phone practically be a third appendage.

"I figured as much."

"How's that?"

"The night she left. We had a fight. It got kind of ugly, the mudslinging back and forth. I would have left it at that, but she decided to fling the phone, too. It got busted up, though I thought they made those things out of titanium these days, so I was hoping it didn't break all the way. Or that she'd gotten it fixed if it had. I know she took it with her because it wasn't on the floor when I came back downstairs. She's got pretty good aim, Shea. If I hadn't ducked, that trace would have led you straight between my eyes."

He could hear Shea laugh on the other end. "A girl that takes after my own heart," she said. "Or my dad's, at least. You think he didn't want a son with a golden left arm, you'd be dead wrong."

Joe watched a squirrel bounding through the grass, into the mulch, and up the front of the tree. It worked itself around to the backside and disappeared from his view. He had a sudden urge to tell Shea the rest of what happened that night with Samantha.

"Well, the Amazin's sure could use one right now," he said, ignoring the urge.

"Yeah, every day since '76."

"So what do you think I should do, Shea? I figured she might replace the thing, turn it back on. Your search would have caught that?"

"Yeah. Even if she used a different SIM card or a new phone. My guy is at the company. He checked it all. And what should you do? Shit, it's hard to say. You call around to her friends?"

He had, though Samantha had recently changed more about herself than just her favorite colors and taste for coffee. A few months back, she started hanging out with a different crowd at school. Artists, mostly. At least that's what she'd told Joe they were. He hadn't pressed her because, well, he didn't think she was preparing to run out on him. And because after so many years working the streets of Newark, the kids out here wouldn't have alarmed him unless they started leaving IEDs along the side of the town's lone main road.

He'd need to do a better job digging them up.

"Listen, Joe, I've got another call. One other thing you might try? Her phone is listed under your account. Check who she'd been talking to recently, see if any patterns emerge or any numbers that might clue you in. Gotta run, though. Let me know if you need anything else, alright?"

"Sure. Thanks, Shea. And let me know how I can pay back the favor."

They hung up.

Joe finished his coffee, but by now it was lukewarm and the bitterness tasted like stomach acid fighting its way up into his throat. He'd spent a few days assuming Samantha was just blowing off steam. Then a few days telling himself not to overreact. But now he felt the cold instinct that something was wrong creeping up the base of his spine.

Outside, a gust of wind blew through the backyard, swaying the rope swing as if a ghost were sitting in the seat.

His little girl was missing.

And maybe not of her own volition.

JOIN THE MAILING LIST

Did you like this story? How about another one for FREE?

Join Niz Thomas' mailing list for alerts as to when the next Ledgerman books are released.

Join now to also get:
FREE STORIES
MEMBER DEALS & DISCOUNTS
FIRST LOOK ACCESS
AUTHOR INTERVIEWS
LIMITED EDITIONS
AND MORE

Join the newsletter here: nizthomas.com/newsletter
Or by sending an email to: niz@nizthomas.com

ALSO BY NIZ THOMAS

For a full list and links to purchase, visit:

NIZTHOMAS.COM/BOOKS

NIZPATCHES

Volume One: Crime Stories

Volume Two: Twisted Crime

NIZ THOMAS COLLECTED

Volume One: Crime Stories

THE LEDGERMAN SERIES

The Omega Diner: A Ledgerman Story

Razor's Edge: A Ledgerman Novel

Thin Air: A Ledgerman Story

Last Ride: A Ledgerman Novel

THE TRUE NAME SERIES

Call Me Betsy

Call Me Gertrude

Call Me Aileen

NOVELS

Family Tree

Door Number Five at the Memory Motel

And The Moon Is Full And Bright

Election Day

SHORT STORIES

A Refraction of Kind Light

A Void of Ascendant Light

Becalm This Mighty Sea

Burn Off

Burn Together

Cheers

Elder Hunger

Fiona's Mercy

First Light of Every Morning

How to Commune with a Futurist

Lady Death

Lane Change

My Bleeding Kansas

No Control

Paint It Thrice

Rail Music

Ray-Ray's Stoop

Recidivist History

Red Tempest

Ships in the Night

Songbird

The Bad Guy

The Climb and The Glory

The Forever-ish Flame War

The Imminent Fire

The Impassable Way

The Light Alone

The Two O'Clock Killer

The Voice of Rage and Ruin

Upon Your Dreams They Prey: A Lullaby

Vanguard

Vida's Sixth Trip Around the Sun

When Sheds Talk

ABOUT THE AUTHOR

Join the mailing list for a FREE short story
website: nizthomas.com/newsletter
email: niz@nizthomas.com

Niz Thomas grew up a fan of *The Silence of the Lambs*, heist movies, and 007. Not surprisingly, as a kid he wanted to be an FBI agent, a cat burglar, and a spy. He decided to go to college instead and has regretted it every day since.

Niz is an eleven-time honoree in the *Writers of the Future* contest, receiving a Finalist designation for his short story *Vida's Sixth Trip Around the Sun* and several Silver Honorable Mention awards. He is also the author of over thirty short stories and several forthcoming novels, including the highly anticipated horror novella *And The Moon Is Full And Bright*, the dark suspense novel *Family Tree*, and the near-future political cat-and-mouse novella, *Election Day*.

Join his mailing list for limited edition story art, early access to new releases, and periodic FREE short stories.

Join the mailing list: nizthomas.com/newsletter